SURVIVAL OF THE FASTEST

Matt shot the man twice in the face and once in the chest. The gunman spun around completely then fell facefirst to the floor.

"I'll be goddamned, Ramsey," Dowd said. "You're one hell of a shot."

Dowd was behind Matt now.

When he stepped forward from the shadows, he put his own gun directly against the back of Matt's skull.

"Drop your gun, Reb, elsewise I'm gonna put a big hole in your head."

"You're done in this town, Dowd, and you know it," Matt told him. "Killing me won't buy you anything."

"Maybe it'll buy me some satisfaction, Reb. If you hadn't come to town, none of this would have happened."

"That's where you're wrong. If it hadn't been me, it would have been somebody else."

"I told you to throw your gun down, Reb."

The lawman eased back on the hammer . . .

BLOOD STORM

WILL McLENNAN

JOVE BOOKS, NEW YORK

BLOOD STORM

A Jove Book / published by arrangement with
the author

PRINTING HISTORY
Jove edition / September 1991

ISBN: 0-515-10668-2

Jove Books are published by The Berkley Publishing Group,
200 Madison Avenue, New York, New York 10016.
The name "JOVE" and the "J" logo
are trademarks belonging to Jove Publications, Inc.

PRINTED IN THE UNITED STATES OF AMERICA

10 9 8 7 6 5 4 3 2 1

BLOOD STORM

TUESDAY

Two days before the robbery and the killings, the nineteen-year-old girl named Jenna Fairbain returned to the place of her birth on a stagecoach.

Matt Ramsey had been the coach's only other passenger for the past day and a half. In that time he'd decided that the pretty but tired-looking girl was being pursued by some mighty deadly demons. Every time she dozed off inside the big Concord coach, she woke up a few minutes later, screaming and sweaty and caught up in the throes of a real frenzy. Matt knew something about nightmares such as these. Following the war, during which time he'd proudly wore the gray of the Confederacy, Matt had been chased by his own demons. He'd often awakened just as Jenna had.

At 10:12 A.M. on the second day, the Concord's two drivers gave the horses some real leather and sent them racing through a rocky pass. At the top of a steep hill, Ramsey had his first look at the town of Templar. On a cold, gray November morning like this one, Templar wasn't pretty at all. Despite a number of large brick homes and a shopping district where there appeared to be at least three buildings of two stories, Templar needed yellow sun and green foliage to look like something more than just a haven from the icy winds that cut down from the jagged mountains surrounding it.

He glanced over at Jenna. A curious smile had touched her soft, well-shaped lips. This was a smile that held a secret, not a smile of pleasure. She looked at Matt then and said, "It's an ugly place, isn't it?"

"I suppose it's nice in the spring."

She shook her head. "Not even then."

Matt didn't know what to say. An angry edge had come into the girl's voice. He knew she didn't want him to argue.

She sank back into the seat. The coach tossed and heaved as the horses raced down the last hill before reaching the town itself. The interior smelled of cigar smoke and perfume and sweat.

She raised her head then and once again looked out at the town. This time there was no smile, no anger. This time there was only an expression of quiet sorrow in her huge blue eyes.

Matt wondered what could have made her so sad. She looked too young for this kind of grief.

"You've been a pleasant traveling companion, Mr. Ramsey, and I appreciate it. You're a true gentleman."

"Thank you."

"I only wish there were more like you in this world." She had a very formal way of speaking, careful to pronounce each word.

All Matt could think of was how actresses spoke from a stage.

"I hope you enjoy your stay here," Matt said.

"Oh, I will. You can be sure of that." And once more the smile of secrecy was on her mouth. This time her eyes looked happy, too. "If you don't mind, I'd like to give you a small memento of our time together."

Matt thought her words were strange, but he shrugged and said, "Sure."

She reached into her leather valise, rummaged about for a few seconds, and then pulled a single sheet of white paper from inside. She held up the printed side of the paper for Matt to see.

Beneath a very good picture of Jenna were the words "JENNA FAIRBAIN, Actress Extraordinaire."

So she *was* an actress.

With a pen that seemed to appear from nowhere, Jenna quickly wrote something on the back of the paper. She then handed the page to Matt.

"To Matt, a gentleman in a world of scoundrels."

Once more Matt was struck by the ferocity of her feelings. Given her young age, her bitterness was considerable.

"Templar!" the stage driver shouted down from above.

"Please keep that and think of me sometimes," Jenna said.

"Don't worry. I will."

"And I'll think of you, too."

He smiled. She still made him uneasy, though he wasn't quite sure why.

The stage pulled up to the depot, a stable boy bundled up in a flannel jacket and earmuffs already running for the horses that would need to be changed.

Jenna got up to go, but as she did so, the coach gave one last shudder and her still-open valise pitched forward, throwing its contents onto Matt's seat.

Most of the stuff was about what you'd expect to find in a young woman's valise: underthings and skin preparations and blouses and skirts and a pair of high-button shoes.

Next to Matt's left hand sat something you didn't

expect to find in her valise, however: a .44 much like Matt's own.

With a delicate hand, Jenna reached across and retrieved the gun. As she set the .44 back inside her valise, she said, "I just don't like going places unarmed these days."

"Don't blame you."

But she looked nervous and sounded defensive, which only made Matt all the more curious.

The stage driver opened the door and put out a hand for Jenna to take as she stepped down.

She said no more to Matt—didn't even turn around for a final good-bye. She just kept on moving ahead, as if he'd discovered something that had embarrassed her.

He kept thinking about the demons that troubled her sleep and the big, deadly .44 she kept in her valise.

Then he stepped down from the stage and forgot about her as he took his first good look at Templar.

The snow that would later turn into a blizzard had just now started falling.

CHAPTER

★ **1** ★

The funny thing was, you never thought of doctors dying. Somewhere in the back of your mind, they were somehow an immortal breed.

But die they did. Matt had seen several medicos die during the final years of the war: three from consumption and an equal number from gunshot wounds.

Now, six hours after he'd stepped off the Templar stage, Matt again watched a doctor in the process of dying.

Clifton Ruark had been a Confederate surgeon and a damned good one. He'd saved Matt's life on his operating table. After the war, trying like most of his generation to forget all the sights and sounds of that terrible time, Ruark had drifted west with his proper little southern wife, and together they'd started a decent life for themselves here in Utah, up near Bear Lake on the Idaho border.

The room Matt sat in was hushed and shadowy, a kerosene lantern turned low the only light. In the double bed across from Matt's armchair lay a white-haired man snoring gently. Matt could hardly believe this was Clifton. Though the surgeon was four years Matt's jun-

5

ior, he looked twenty years older. This was what the
cancer had done to the man—and all within the past
nine months according to Winona, Clifton's eighteen-
year-old daughter. In one of those terrible ironies that
are fairly common in life, Essie, Clifton's wife, had
herself died of the cancer two years before.

Matt sat in the chair, drawing on a pipe and looking
at his friend. They were getting at that age now, Matt
supposed. A few deaths in the early forties, and then
more and more of them as the war generation headed
toward its fifties.

"Mr. Ramsey."

She had a sweet, young, slightly scared voice, Winona
Ruark did, especially when she was within sight of her
father. She hadn't yet come to terms with the fact that
she would soon lose him.

Matt looked up. Winona, in a gingham dress and a
white shawl, stood in the darkened doorway and said,
"I've made some dinner for us. Father's sleeping anyway. You may as well eat now."

Matt glanced at his friend again and sighed. He'd
already said a few prayers for Clifton, and tonight, during those cold alien hours when the rest of the world
slumbered, he'd likely be awake, saying a few more.

"I want to thank you again for coming out here."

"My pleasure, Winona."

"Father always said you were one of his best friends,
and now you've proved it."

She put out a good spread: pork chops with fried
potatoes, applesauce, and corn.

They were in the kitchen. It was modern, with a pump
right at the sink and a double-door icebox in the corner.
Light from a Rochester lamp suspended above the table
flickered across their faces.

Winona said Lutheran grace. A Baptist, Matt wasn't sure of the words, so he just bowed his head reverently.

They ate for a time without words, uncomfortable with each other in the way strangers usually are.

Matt didn't want to talk about her father, afraid he'd only make her sad again.

He said, "I had kind of a strange companion on the stagecoach."

"Oh?"

"Young woman name of Jenna."

"Jenna Fairbain?"

He nodded.

"Gosh," Winona said.

"Something wrong?"

Winona thought a moment. "I guess I just never thought she'd ever come back here. After what happened, I mean."

"What happened?"

Winona dropped her gaze. "Uh, somebody . . . hurt her."

"Hurt?"

"You know, Mr. Ramsey. What a man does to a woman against her will."

"Oh."

"She went to the sheriff and to the city council and told them who did it and everything, but they wouldn't believe her. They accused her of spreading lies and they packed her on a stagecoach one day and they told her never to come back."

"When was this?"

"Oh, let's see now. Ten years ago."

"She was nine when it happened?"

Winona looked at him steadily across the flickering lamplight. "Yes."

"You sound as if you believe her."

"I do. And so did—does Father." She caught herself right away, looking both embarrassed and afraid of speaking about her father in the past tense.

"You mean some people doubted that anything had even happened?"

"Mayor Malloy always said that nothing had happened," Winona said. "That she'd made up the whole thing, both the man she accused and the—assault, too."

"You said your father believes her."

"Yes. She came here right after it happened. That's how we know it's true. He examined her. She'd not only been . . . touched, she'd been beaten pretty badly, too."

"But they wouldn't believe your father either?"

She set down her fork and stared at her plate. "I haven't told you about her father."

"Oh?"

"He was generally considered the worst man in town. A drunkard and a thief. He spent half his time in jail. I guess that, given her father, people didn't much care what happened to Jenna."

"That isn't a good reason to run her out of town."

Winona smiled. "You've never heard Mayor Malloy when he gets going. He's got a saying: 'The sun don't shine unless you're smiling.' Which is his way of saying that bad news breeds more bad news. In the scheme of things, neither Jenna nor her father are very important to this town. So even if something did happen to Jenna . . ." She shook her head. "I wish for her sake she'd never come back here."

"You don't think they'll accept her?"

"No. Templar is a very self-righteous town, Matt. It's the one thing my father could never accept about it. How unforgiving it is."

Matt sipped his coffee. "She became an actress."

"That's what I heard. Word drifted back, I mean. Folks here said 'actress' was just another way of saying 'whore.' "

"Seems like if anybody should be mad it should be Jenna. She's the wronged party here."

Winona laughed again. This time there was sadness in the sound. "Oh, you've got some things to learn about Templar, Matt. You surely do."

Then she went and got them two pieces of rhubarb pie.

She'd taken the room all the way at the end of the hall. There was a door bolt but she still wasn't satisfied. She pushed a chair up under the doorknob. Let somebody try to get in now.

She lay in perfect darkness.

With a bad storm already in progress, the hotel was filled with people. Laughter, coughing, talking, cursing— all the familiar sounds pressed at the walls on either side of her and threatened to smash them in.

Perfect darkness—absolutely still, arms at sides, eyes shut tight. She was rehearsing for her own burial some day. She had done this ever since she was a little girl, even before she'd been raped and beaten.

Perfect darkness. Eternal.

She wondered if Tony and Steve were in town yet. They weren't supposed to look her up till morning. She hoped Tony didn't get drunk and spoil their plans.

Oh, yes, their plans. Nine years now she'd had this dream. She would descend on his house and terrify him. And then she would steal the only things worth stealing: his gold, his diamonds, his greenbacks.

He had nothing else worth taking.

Then she would go to South America. She had seen

photographs of Brazil—and paintings, too—in New York. Colors beyond imagining, soft and summery colors of flowers and pretty dresses and the eyes of beautiful women.

Wind came and rattled the windows, and snow blew against the panes like buckshot.

She was a long, long way from Brazil, up here in the ragged bitter mountains of her birth.

She thought again of Tony and Steve. She supposed they were outlaws, though she'd never chosen to think of them that way, two young drifters who'd befriended her after a particularly grueling dramatic performance in a rather violent mining town. Both swore they could do what she wanted. Both swore they could get in and scare him and steal his things, yet not do any permanent harm to him. None of them wanted to be pursued by the law the rest of their lives. But she wondered. She'd seen Tony's temper.

Perfect darkness.

She put her hands at her sides and closed her eyes again. Sometimes images of that night came back to her. How he'd slapped her. And how he'd put himself into her in the roughest way possible. And how she'd bitten his lower lip. And how he'd left her there on the back porch, sobbing.

She'd gone home then and told her father all about it. He'd then done something she'd never suspected him capable of: He'd picked up his ancient muzzleloader and set off to defend the honor and virtue of his only daughter.

To kill the sonofabitch, as he'd said.

But he hadn't come home till dawn, and then he was staggering drunk and had fallen down on the floor next to her cot, and she'd seen the green scraps of money sticking out from his shirt pocket. She didn't have to ask where the money had come from, nor why he'd been given it.

He hadn't shot the man. He probably hadn't even raised his voice.

Not after the man had waved crackling greenbacks in his face. Liquor money.

So all these years later she lay in the darkness of this hotel room, wondering if she'd ever feel happy or peaceful or normal or proper. If there'd ever be a day when she didn't loathe and despise herself so much.

Maybe after they descended on the old man's house and she got the satisfaction of watching pure cold fear take him over. Maybe then she'd feel good about herself.

Maybe then.

She listened to the wind and tried to cry, but she was long shut of tears. Long shut of them.

There was only hatred now, and it was bitter milk for suckling.

CHAPTER

★2★

Clifton was still asleep when Matt, shaved and washed up and wearing clean clothes, sat down to breakfast next morning. Winona fixed him two eggs, toast, potatoes, strawberry jam, and black coffee—strong, the way he liked it. Then she excused herself, saying she had to spend much of the morning working in the cellar, finishing off some canning. Two or three times during their conversation she glanced eastward, in the direction of her father's bedroom. Clearly she meant to keep herself busy. It wasn't much to put up against death, keeping busy, but sometimes it was the only way a human being could keep herself from going crazy.

As Matt ate his solitary breakfast, he read the local paper, which spent much of its front page bragging about the fact that the town of Templar was now twenty years old and that it boasted "eight brick buildings on Main Street, a school, four churches, three hotels, two restaurants, a brewery, several sawmills, an iron foundry, and about forty stores and shops." There was also a library that held "more than 600 books."

As he finished eating, Matt decided that Winona had the right idea. Sitting around the house and waiting for

Clifton to come out of his coma for a while was too depressing. He needed to do something.

He decided to take a close-up look at Templar and see just how accurate the self-congratulatory newspaper article really was.

An inch of snow had fallen overnight. The white stuff lent the town and the surrounding mountains a gentleness it otherwise lacked.

Because Christmas wasn't far away now, brightly decorated store windows added color to the overcast day, and wagons and surreys and sleighs with bells on them jingled through the streets.

In all, Matt spent half an hour walking the streets. By the time he'd finished, he had to agree with the newspaper writer that Templar was a pretty impressive place, especially given its location, so high up in the ragged mountains.

By now his cheeks and nose were cold. He wanted to sit down in a warm place and have some coffee.

Choosing a "CAFE" sign at random, he took his hat off and went inside. The place smelled of grease and cigarette smoke.

Near a back booth, a small crowd of angry women stood in a semicircle. One of them was leaning down and talking to somebody in the booth, though Matt couldn't see who. The woman sounded on the verge of swearing. She kept saying "You had no right! No right at all!" At this point the other ladies, bundled up in town-fancy winter clothes, would nod their heads solemnly as if they were judges passing an angry verdict on somebody.

From the kitchen, finally, came a big man with a bald head and one of the longest walrus-style mustaches Matt had ever seen. He was dressed in a grease-spattered white shirt, apron, and gray work trousers. He carried a mean-looking meat cleaver that he held weaponlike in his right hand.

He went over to the small crowd of women and said, "That's enough, ladies. You've had your say. Now I'm asking you to get out."

One of the women said to the cook, "You shouldn't even be serving her here."

"It's my place," the big man said, "and I can do any damn thing I want to in it."

This clearly displeased the ladies, who huffed and puffed about the dearth of gentlemanly behavior in this town and who went back briefly to glaring at the person in the booth. It was easy enough to guess that the husbands of these women were bankers and lawyers and politicians.

The big man said again, "I've told you now, ladies, you've had your say and I'd appreciate it if you'd leave."

Another of the ladies put her hands on her formidable hips and said, "Don't expect to see us in here again."

"I guess I'll just have to live with a broken heart," the man said, and he flashed a surprisingly boyish grin to whomever sat in the booth.

The ladies left. Their exit was noisy and dramatic and took much longer than it should have, but finally they were gone.

Now Matt saw who was in the booth.

Even with her head angled downward, Matt could see the silver tears in her eyes. It was Jenna.

Matt hadn't taken a seat yet. The big man glared at him, as if Matt had been with that contingent of proper town ladies who'd just left.

"You want something, friend?" the big man asked.

"I was hoping I could get a cup of coffee."

Jenna looked up then and saw Matt. "He's a friend of mine, Earle. Treat him right."

Jealousy played in Earle's gaze as he looked first at Jenna, then at Matt. "A friend, huh?"

Jenna caught his implication. "That's right, Earle, a friend. And that's all." She nodded toward Matt. "He rode in with me on the stage and he was a perfect gentleman."

The big man's glower began to fade. He put out a big hard slab of a hand that dwarfed Matt's. They shook.

"I'm Earle Wiley."

"Matt Ramsey."

"Sorry about spouting off. I'm just a little tired of people giving Jenna here a bad time."

Matt smiled. "Was that the town temperance league?"

Earle laughed. His teeth weren't too good and he was a long way from pretty, but he had a comfortable masculine presence that made people like him. "I guess I get a little overprotective where Jenna's concerned."

"Don't blame you. She's a nice young woman."

Without hesitating, Earle said, "I'm going to marry her."

Matt looked at Jenna. She dropped her gaze.

Trying to sound lighthearted, Earle said, "I've been wanting to marry her ever since she was ten years old. And one of these days she's going to take me serious." With that, he wiped his meat cleaver on his apron and started back toward the kitchen. "How do you like your coffee?"

"Black."

"Black it is then." He nodded toward Jenna. "Why don't you sit down and keep her company."

Earle went to the back.

"He's a nice man," Jenna said.

"He seems like it."

She smiled bleakly. "But I'm not going to marry him."

"You could do worse."

She shook her head. "I'm not going to marry anybody." Once again there was an edge to her words. He thought of what it must have been like for a young girl to be raped. She'd probably want nothing to do with men, and he couldn't blame her.

Matt changed the subject. "Do you always attract a following?"

"Those women?"

"Right."

She frowned. "They don't feel I have any right to come back here. They're afraid of me."

"Why?"

"I'm sure Winona told you about what happened to me."

"She likes you."

"I know. And I like her. Anyway, those women are afraid that one of their husbands is the man who raped me."

"You mean they don't know for sure?"

"I only gave the name to the mayor and the sheriff. And as far as I know, they've never told anybody. They're protecting him." She sighed. "So they're not happy to see me. I'm bringing up the past all over again. Plus I'm an actress, which they think is the next worst thing to being an out-and-out whore."

Earle brought two cups of steaming black coffee.

"So'd you figure out a date yet?" he asked Jenna.

"Not yet, Earle."

"A month from now would be nice. Christmastime." Earle winked at Matt. "I'm a sentimental guy. I like Christmas marriages."

Jenna smiled. "If I actually said yes you'd run for the hills, Earle."

He dropped all jocularity and stared straight at her. "Give me a try, kid, and I'll show you how wrong you are."

And with that, trailing a slight air of melancholy, Earle went back to his kitchen.

Over the next twenty minutes, the cafe began to fill up, as miners and merchants alike took the place over.

Jenna and Matt talked about a variety of things. Sometimes she seemed friendly, almost trusting of him, and then she'd abruptly pull back, cold and suspicious. He thought again of how being raped must have affected her attitude about men.

She looked up at the big Benrus wall clock and said, "I've got to go, Matt. Sorry."

"That's all right. I've enjoyed our cup of coffee."

"Me too."

"And for what it's worth, I still think you should take Earle up on his offer."

"I'll think about it, Matt. I really will."

Then she was gone. Matt sat there with his cup of coffee, taking his pipe out and getting some good strong drags on it. Earle came over. "She say where she's going?"

"Afraid not."

"I'm not being nosy, Matt. I just worry about her."

Matt nodded. "So do I, Earle. So do I."

His name was Tony Jessup and he had spent six of his twenty-two years in prison for cutting a man's throat with a Bowie knife. His age had saved him from hanging, but no amount of imprisonment would change his basic penchant for violence. Indeed, prison had only made him all the more formidable as a killer.

Tony's dark good looks had always been his salvation. While he wasn't boyish in any way, there was a curious gentleness in his brown eyes and in the quiet way he spoke. Most people just didn't believe a truly violent man could be like this.

Now as he sat his horse on a shelf of rock above the town of Templar, Tony Jessup nodded to his partner, Steve Moore, and said, "I've got a good feeling about this place."

Steve, chunky, blond, neither attractive nor particularly smart, said, "I just don't want to get in no bad trouble, Tony."

Steve had been Tony's cellmate for the last two years of Tony's term. Steve was an ideal companion for Tony, because he was willing to obey Tony almost without complaint. He could only envy Tony his looks, his charm, and his cunning. Steve had been serving time for barn burning. A farmer had beaten Steve's father in a saloon brawl and Steve had wanted to pay the man back. The abiding irony was that when Steve's father learned what his somewhat stupid son had done, he got his razor strop and savagely beat the boy himself.

"You hungry?" Steve asked.

Tony smiled. "You've got some stomach, Steve."

"I eat when I get scared."

"I know. But there's nothing to be scared of. It's going to be easy for us. We ride in and we ride out, and that's all there'll be to it." Tony looked back down the ragged, snow-covered mountain that slanted toward the town below. From up here everything was in miniature, including the small red train depot and the racing black locomotive.

He glanced back at the worried-looking Steve. Actually, Tony believed his own words. This should be a simple job. There was a rich old man in this town who kept a lot of money and valuables in his house. Jenna knew who he was and where he lived. The three of them would go in, tie the old man up, take his stuff, and head out of town fast.

And then Tony would be shut of Jenna, too. They'd been lovers for the past year, ever since he'd seen her pathetic dramatic performance in a cheap tavern on the northern edge of Wyoming. If she hadn't been so difficult to seduce, he'd have probably dropped her long before. He usually had little trouble. But getting into Jenna's knickers had taken months of hard work. And it hadn't really been worth all the trouble. She was a timid, clinging little girl really, and not much else. The night he'd finally gotten around to telling her good-bye, she surprised him by telling him about the man who'd raped her and how she wanted to go back to Templar and steal everything of value he possessed. This sounded too good to pass up.

So now here they were.

"Be good to see Jenna again, huh, Tony?"

"Oh, yes. Real good." Tony smirked.

"I'm glad you're bein' nice to her again."

Tony looked over at him in disbelief. Jenna was protective of Steve, so Steve became, in some sickening way, her own big baby. He blubbered about Jenna constantly. One of the few times he'd ever spoken harshly to Tony was on a night that Jenna had been left in tears.

"I shoulda brought her a gift," Steve said.

"Yeah," Tony said, keeping up the sarcasm that was lost on Steve, "so should I."

Then he reined up his horse and turned the roan toward the narrow, snowy road that wound down the mountain to the town.

It was going to be so easy, Tony thought. So damned easy.

CHAPTER

★3★

The last time he'd slapped her, she'd threatened to quit if he ever laid a hand on her again.

So this afternoon, just after he finished bringing his big, wrinkled hand down across the right side of her jaw, Carmody stood his ground and glared at her, as if daring her to say something.

She did not give him the satisfaction of crying.

She did not even give him the satisfaction of whimpering.

She just bowed her head and took in a great deal of breath quickly. He sensed but did not see a shudder pass through her frail Indian body.

Tenana her name was, and she'd been his maid since he'd been banished from New Hampshire by his wealthy father and sent out west to "become something resembling a man."

In the beginning, of course—just after he'd had local Indians drag native stone from nearby rivers and ponds and build this huge mansion of his—he'd slept with her. But soon enough—he was this way with all women; it was a curse—he tired of her physically. She lost all privilege and became just one more person for him to order around. And to slap on occasion, as he saw fit.

"I specifically asked for lemon in this tea."

She raised her head.

She was unable to hide the tears that moistened her eyes. They gave him a small measure of the pain he'd inflicted anyway.

"Yes, sir," she said, her head still bowed.

He looked at her now and wondered how he'd ever managed to sleep with her. She was all dried up. Even her breasts had shrunk. In her beaded rawhide dress, her little beer belly sticking out, her black hair thinning on top, she seemed to be a ghoul of some kind.

It was definitely time he got himself a new maid.

"Will that be all, sir?"

"Yes. But next time listen carefully to what I say."

"Yes, sir."

She had a daughter who was sick. She needed the white man's medicine. Tenana couldn't quit, even if she'd wanted to. Her maid's job was all she had for the medicine.

She left the room, and he went back to his desk.

He sat staring out at the snowy sloping hills. Fir trees clung to the steep sides of these hills. In the distance, he could see three children playing on red sleds. Earlier they'd built a snowman, an icon of ice and snow that now seemed to watch over the entire valley.

How the hell had he ever gotten to be forty-eight goddamn years old anyway?

This had lately become his obsession, his age. He noticed that young women were no longer so impressed with him. He'd always had a sense of his own hand-someness—"He's too damned pretty for his own good!" his father had always bellowed at his mother—but now that sense was gone. When he tried to ingratiate himself with young women now, he sensed only that he was a pathetic beast.

The hair was no longer merely streaked with gray; it was nearly white. And the jawline was lost to excess flesh. And beneath the startling blue eyes were small gray pouches that no amount of sleep took away.

He was old. Not ancient, certainly; not some old cuss who doddered his way up the center aisle at church on Sunday mornings and made all the youngsters giggle. But he was old in the sense that he was no longer young. And never would be again.

What the hell had happened, he wondered as he gazed out on the gentle wintry scene. He felt as if some dark force had tricked or betrayed him out of his youth.

And then he saw the woman on the road below. She stood in the center of the road and stared straight up at his house, as if she knew exactly where he was and exactly what he was doing.

He rejected the notion that it was Jenna.

My god, she'd been pushed from this town years ago and told never to come back.

No, Jenna was impossible.

Still, images from that night came back to him. Her pleas; her screams. The pain of him inside her. And then slapping her again and again to stop her hysterical tears afterward.

Bitch.

So how was it, all these long years later, that she came to stand in the center of the road below his mansion, gazing up at him like a phantom?

No. Impossible. It couldn't be Jenna.

Couldn't be . . .

But even as he stood there denying what he saw in the overcast shadows of the glum, cold afternoon, he knew that it was in fact Jenna standing down there.

Jenna had come back.

As she'd promised that long-ago night.

Come back for him.

"I'm afraid I'm not much of a host, Matt."

"I'm just glad to see you, my friend."

Clifton had been awake for the past hour. He sat propped up in his bed in the room that smelled of medicine and death. He was pale and frail in a way that was painful for Matt to see.

Matt watched his friend spoon broth into his mouth. Some of it ran down the front of his robe. He didn't seem to notice. Every once in a while, Clifton would look at Matt with his sick scared eyes and put a quick little smile on his face.

Clifton's room was snug. There was a small stove in the corner. Snow was accumulating on the windowsills. And in the distance, children laughed as they slid down a steep hill.

Winona came in and took the tray from her father's lap. "Don't let him talk you into playing hearts, Matt."

"Oh?"

"He cheats."

Matt laughed. "That sounds like something Clifton would do. Cheat at a high-paying game like that."

Clifton smiled again. "Actually, Matt, it's true. I do cheat. You know my ego. I always hated to lose."

Matt noted how not only Winona but now even Clifton spoke of himself in the past tense.

"Just don't take advantage of him, father," Winona said brightly as she left the room. "After all, he's our guest."

Clifton put his head back and closed his eyes. The cancer had sapped him thoroughly. He was probably sinking into sleep again.

Matt got up and went to the window. Kids in snow were always fun to watch, their long scarves trailing in the wind behind them, the bulky movements of their bodies buried beneath all those winter clothes. Hell, even at his age, sliding down a hill would probably be fun.

"Matt."

When he turned around, he saw that Clifton had opened his blue eyes again.

Clifton said, "Would you come over here and sit down again?"

"Sure."

When he was seated, Matt said, "Don't feel obligated to talk, Clifton. If you want to doze off, go ahead."

"There's something I need to talk to you about."

"All right."

From somewhere within his covers, Clifton produced a plain white envelope. On the front of it, in Clifton's blunt, unmistakable penmanship, was written "SHERIFF'S OFFICE."

"Have you met Sheriff Dowd yet?"

"Afraid I haven't," Matt said.

Clifton smiled. "Remember old Sergeant Carver?"

"Sure."

"How he never wanted to make any decisions or be responsible for anything?"

Matt laughed at the recollection. "Right."

"Well, that's how Dowd is. That's how he's hung on to his sheriffing job for the past ten years. There are three men who run this town, and he lets them make all the decisions. He just does what they tell him."

"Nice arrangement."

Clifton smiled again. "That way you don't make anybody mad."

Clifton took the letter and placed it in Matt's hand. "Winona said you rode in on the stage with Jenna."

"Yes."

"And Winona also told me that you know what happened to Jenna."

"Right."

Clifton's blue eyes narrowed. "You should have seen her that night, Matt. She didn't quit trembling for almost an entire day."

"She'd been badly beaten too?"

"Very badly."

"But nobody would do anything about it?"

"Certainly not Sheriff Dowd, Matt. There was no way he was going to confront George Carmody."

"That's the man who raped her?"

Clifton nodded. "And the richest man in town."

"I take it he's one of the three men who give Dowd his orders."

"Exactly."

"And you want me to give this envelope to him?"

"Oh no. Not to Dowd," Clifton said. "To his deputy, William Wisdom."

"That's some name, Wisdom."

"Isn't it, though?" Clifton tapped the envelope that now lay on the bed between them. "Wisdom's young, but he's got some fire. Nobody's ever told him what happened that night. Hell, Bill was eight years old when it happened. The letter tells him everything, including the fact that I swear as a physician that Jenna was indeed raped and that she didn't make up her story."

"Can he do anything about it?"

"The time limit on prosecution hasn't run out, if that's what you mean."

Matt shook his head. "You think a kid deputy will risk his job to take on the most important man in town?"

"Maybe he will if you talk to him. You can be a mighty persuasive fellow, Matt."

And then Clifton fell to coughing.

Matt had to look away from the pain he saw and heard in his old friend. It wouldn't be long now.

"Sonofabitch," Clifton said after his coughing had subsided. "You'd think that with all the sickness I was around in my life I could've handled all this a little better." He looked at Matt. "But you know what? I'm just as scared and just as depressed as all my patients were."

"I reckon I will be too," Matt said.

Another coughing fit ensued, but it ended quickly.

"Take the envelope, Matt, and look up Wisdom, all right?"

"All right."

"I don't know what Jenna's doing back here, but it makes me nervous."

"Why?"

"I'm not sure. I just don't think she'd come back unless it was for some kind of vengeance." He shook his head. "I don't know what she's got in mind, but I doubt that it's very good news for anybody in these parts. I can't tell you how bitter she was that nobody would do anything about her being raped and beaten. And hell, who can blame her? I'd be bitter too." He looked up at Matt. "She deserves a good life, Matt. She spent all her young years putting up with that alcoholic father of hers, and then somebody rapes her and the town won't do a damn thing about it. I just want to stop her before she does anything that'll make her life even more of a mess."

"Is Wisdom usually around the office?"

"No. He's out and about most of the time. Right about now he's probably sitting in the Excelsior Cafe, having a beef sandwich and three cups of coffee. He has the same thing every day. The waitresses all laugh about it.

Wisdom's real popular with the common folk in town. If he could ever get out from under Dowd . . ."

Exhaustion claimed him again. His head sank back in the pillows. His complexion was paler than ever. Breathing was labored now, and sweat covered his face.

"Anything I can get you?" Matt asked.

"Just see that Jenna finally gets her due," Clifton said.

Matt leaned over and patted Clifton's hand. "I'll take care of it for you, my friend. I promise."

Jenna was just leaving her hotel when she saw him.

Striding down the street. Buried inside a huge new suede greatcoat. Homburg tilted at a rakish angle. Dollar cigar trailing blue smoke in the gray morning.

George Carmody, the man who'd raped her.

For years she'd dreamed of this moment, planned for it, the time when she saw him again.

How sweet her vengeance would be. How bold she'd act, walking right up to him and telling him how much she hated him for what he'd done.

But now that the actual moment was here, all she did was stand and stare at him, watching him work his arrogant way down the crowded boardwalk.

Her impressions: He was older, heavier, no longer the spoiled, handsome boy-man he'd been. She hadn't been prepared for this. In memory, he'd remained the perfect villain, his sleek good looks only making him all the more villainous. But somehow he was a different person, with the excess weight and the white hair and the jowls padding his jawline.

But then the images of that night returned. How afraid she'd been. How he'd pushed himself into her despite her physical agony. How afterward he'd hurt her with his fists, as if violence to him were as important as the sexual thrills.

And now he didn't look any different at all to her.

Oh, time might have changed his appearance a little, but beneath it all, he was still the same man who'd raped and beaten her.

He vanished into the crowd then.

She stood in the hotel doorway, gathering herself up after the shock of seeing him. Finally her breathing became regular again and the tingle in her fingers left and the knotting in her stomach settled down.

Her plan was intact, and she was going to go through with it. Thanks to George Carmody, she was going to leave the town of Templar a very well-fixed young woman.

She looked at the clock in the jewelry-store window.

Tony and Steve were late, but she knew they would be here soon.

And tonight it would come true at last. The night she'd waited for all these years.

Wisdom liked the respect he got. No doubt about that. He liked walking into the Excelsior and seeing the faces of women light up at his sudden appearance. He liked walking into the Excelsior and having men of every sort pat him on the back and grin like little kids. Wisdom's father had left home when he was seven years old, and he was raised then by a mother who did not care much for men, her lone son included. She died of scarlet fever when Wisdom was nine. He lived with various town families after that, sort of a floating orphanage arrangement. He quit school in the fourth grade and went to work at the sawmill for thirty cents an hour and a twenty-dollar bonus come Christmastime.

Then one day he quit, just like that, and went up to Sheriff Dowd and said, "Town's big enough that you need another deputy, don't you think?" And damned if

Dowd hadn't agreed and gone to the three men who ran the town and said he needed another deputy, and damned if they didn't get him one.

All this history rode on Wisdom's back as he walked into the Excelsior for lunch.

Women smiled; men waved.

He took his usual place at the counter, and instantly a cup of steaming coffee appeared and was set down next to his big raw hand.

As usual, Sissy was his waitress. A fifteen-year-old with pigtails and the cutest nose he'd ever seen, Sissy had a painful crush on the young lawman, and for this reason Wisdom never flirted with her. He didn't want to make her infatuation any more painful than it already was.

"Don't you love this snow?" she asked.

"It's right nice."

"You know what I love to do, Wisdom?" That was everybody's name for him: Wisdom.

"What?"

"Stand outside and stick my tongue out and let the snowflakes fall on it. You ever eaten snow?"

"When I was a kid."

"It tastes great, snow does."

He grinned. "You're right. It does."

She put on a fake scowl. "Oh, I forgot. No self-respectin' deputy would want to be seen standin' outside eatin' snow, would he?"

He kept on grinning. "Don't reckon he would." He looked up at the chalkboard with the day's special. The stew sounded damned good and he ordered it.

"Myron did a real good job. You'll like it," she said before leaving. Myron was the cook. Sissy was always honest with customers, telling them when he did good and when he did bad.

Wisdom sat there and drank his coffee, a short, intense young man with curly dark hair and soft blue eyes shadowed only slightly with ancient pain. He was blocky, which meant he'd probably have to fight a paunch when he got into his thirties, but he was also fierce and muscular, one of those men who genuinely enjoyed getting into a good brawl.

For the next few minutes, he sat there returning all the greetings of the people in the cafe. No doubt about it, Wisdom was popular. And he should be. Sheriff Dowd barely spoke to people, and he certainly never listened to their problems. That sort of thing he left to Wisdom, and Wisdom in fact was good with people. Given his own upbringing, he knew that life could be hard for folks and that they needed help sometimes. And people sensed his desire to help them and appreciated it.

"Mr. Wisdom?"

When he looked up, Wisdom saw a slender man with a hard face standing there. He wore a sheepskin jacket and a white Stetson. His face bespoke a quiet intelligence, and knuckle-busted hands hinted at a history of taking care of himself.

"Howdy," Wisdom said.

"My name's Ramsey."

Wisdom and Matt shook hands. "Nice to meet you, Mr. Ramsey."

"I'm here visiting Doctor Ruark."

Wisdom shook his head. "The poor man. It'd be merciful if he'd die soon."

Matt sighed. "We were good friends in the war. I just want his going to be peaceful."

"Don't blame you."

Matt reached inside his sheepskin jacket and produced a long white envelope. "He asked me to give you this."

"Me? If it's official business, Sheriff Dowd probably better see it first."

"Sheriff Dowd would just tear it up."

For the first time Wisdom became curious about what the envelope might contain. "Why don't you sit down, Mr. Ramsey."

"You think we could take a booth? It'd be more private."

"Sure."

Wisdom asked a passing waitress if they could have a booth. She hurried to clean one of them, and the men sat down.

Matt sipped his coffee and rolled a cigarette while Wisdom read the letter.

When he was finished, Wisdom folded the letter and set it down on the table. "That's a pretty serious accusation."

"I know."

"He really thinks that Sheriff Dowd refused to help the girl?"

"He knows Dowd refused to help her."

"I always heard that Jenna left town under mysterious circumstances, but I was never sure what they were. Just that an awful lot of people were glad to see her go."

"She's back now."

"So I've heard," Wisdom said.

"And it's time the town made things right with her. As much as they can, I mean."

Wisdom looked at the hard man across from him. "How do you fit into this, Mr. Ramsey?"

"Given Clifton's condition, I guess I've been elected to see that Jenna gets treated right."

"I get the notion that you can handle yourself pretty well."

"I do all right, I suppose."

"You'll need to. Sheriff Dowd's got two other deputies who're cousins of his. There isn't anything they like to do better than beat up people that the sheriff doesn't like."

Matt frowned. "I like Dowd less and less the more I hear about him."

Wisdom leaned forward, speaking confidentially. "Wish I could say something in his behalf, but the truth is he's a mean, crooked, selfish sonofabitch."

Matt grinned. "But other than that you like him."

Wisdom grinned back. "Other than that I like him a whole lot."

Matt nodded toward the letter. "What're you going to do with that?"

"Present him with it."

"And then what?"

"See how he reacts."

"Most likely he'll run right to the man who raped her."

"Most likely."

"Anything you can do about it?"

Wisdom sipped some of his own coffee. "We've got a county attorney here who'd like nothing more than to put Dowd and his cousins behind bars. With this letter as Doctor Ruark's testimony, I think I can interest the county attorney in moving in on Dowd."

"Won't that be dangerous for you?"

"The truth is, Mr. Ramsey, Dowd and I had to have a showdown sometime anyway. Personally, I'm getting kind of tired waiting for it to happen."

Matt set down his coffee cup. "You sure?"

"I'm sure."

"I'll be staying at the Ruarks' if you need any help."

"I'm sure I'll have to take you up on that, Mr. Ramsey. Dowd sure isn't going to go away peacefully."

"I'm ready," Matt said. "You just let me know when."

And with that he stood up, shook the deputy's hand, straightened his Stetson, and walked out of the cafe.

Wisdom had the feeling that Matt Ramsey was just as good as his word. If it came to gunplay, Matt Ramsey would be right there with him.

CHAPTER

★4★

Tony and Steve went to the livery stable, where an Indian boy took their horses to the back of the barn to rub them down and feed them and board them for the day and night.

They then went on a small tour of the town.

Tony saw right away that Jenna hadn't misled them. The store windows were filled with expensive clothes, the average citizen looked a lot better kept and better dressed than you found in most frontier towns, and when they peeked in the bank window they saw a Mosler safe the size of a small mountain.

Jenna had said that Templar served the entire region, farms and mining outposts alike, and that it was prosperous beyond the hopes of most other towns.

So Tony and Steve walked up and down the board streets, fancying virtually everything they saw, Tony with a good dime cigar tucked in his mouth, Steve with a sharp eye out for Jenna's gift.

"Lookee," Steve said, tugging on Tony's arm like a kid.

"What?"

"The window there."

"What about it?"

"That scarf. The red one."

Tony peered into the store window and sighed. Steve was determined to get Jenna a scarf. At first he started to object, but then he thought: When this is all over and I've got the money, I'm going to take everything and leave anyway. All they'll have is each other. And this damn red scarf.

"She'll really like it," Tony said, feeling almost sorry for Steve and his awkward, embarrassing feelings for Jenna.

Steve sensed Tony's mood—a rare moment of charity. He stared at Tony. "You know I like Jenna, don't you?"

"Sure I do."

"The three of us are good friends, aren't we, Tony?"

"You bet, Steve," Tony said.

"Best friends?"

"That's right. Best friends."

So Steve, gloating with the happy moment, went inside and bought the red scarf.

Tony stayed on the boardwalk, watching people. And it was then that he got his first glimpse of the law in this town.

A heavy man in a black three-piece suit wearing a somewhat theatrical white Stetson came charging down the boardwalk. He had a pair of fancy silver Colts tied low across his beer belly and he carried a Remington carbine in his gloved right hand. He walked with a chunky determination that apparently frightened people, because they sure scurried out of his way when they saw him coming. They seemed mesmerized by the big silver sheriff's star he wore on his lapel. He appeared to be one mean sonofabitch—and that, of course, was exactly the impression he was trying to convey.

Tony didn't move.

He knew he was supposed to move, he knew he probably should move, but he didn't move.

This was a free country, and if he wanted to stand in the middle of a free public sidewalk and gawk at all the citizens, then that was his prerogative.

He'd been pushed around too much in his young life, first by a father too ready with a razor strop, then by assorted deputies and sheriffs eager to break the spirit of a high-spirited young man, and then by prison guards who took unending delight in hitting him with clubs whenever they got the chance.

No, Tony was sick of being pushed around, and he'd be damned if some rube sheriff was going to force him off the boardwalk.

So Tony stood in the exact center of the walk and pretended not to see the man coming at all.

The citizens who'd stepped aside all saw what was about to happen. They looked very nervous.

And then the sheriff was there, plowing right into Tony, hitting him so hard that he literally lifted him off the boardwalk and knocked him back against the shop.

Tony almost fell down.

As he was struggling for balance, the sheriff stopped and said, "Didn't you see me coming?"

"No sir."

"You stood there and watched me."

Tony realized that at least ten citizens were watching the two of them. "It may have looked that way, but I didn't see you."

"You got any idea who am I, kid?"

A couple of the citizens snickered. They were starting to enjoy this now. It was never funny when the sheriff bullied you or somebody you cared about, but

it could be downright hilarious when the sheriff bullied
a stranger.

"You're the sheriff."

"Sheriff Dowd, to be exact."

"Sheriff Dowd then."

"And around here people pay me the respect due my
badge."

With these words, the sheriff's chest seemed to swell
out.

"You understand that?"

"Yes sir."

Now was the time to be polite and subservient, as
he'd already made his point. Tony hadn't yielded the
sidewalk to this lard-ass, hick-town lawman. But from
here on there was nothing to be gained by being belligerent. Tony just wanted to get his money and get out
of town.

"Where you from?" Dowd asked.

For the first time Tony wondered if he hadn't made
a mistake. Sometimes he acted before thinking things
through. What if this tub of shit started asking questions
that Tony didn't want to answer? For instance, questions
about being in prison for several years?

"Just passing through," Tony said.

"That don't answer my question."

"Colorado."

"And what'd you do there?"

"Ranch work."

"What kind of ranch work?"

"Rode line, mostly. Did some branding in the sum-
mer."

"What was the name of the outfit?"

This prick was determined to trip him up, Tony
thought. "Box D."

"Never heard of it."

"Pretty small outfit."

"You think you put one over on me, don't you?"

"Sir?"

"You goddamn well saw me."

"No sir."

"You saw me and you decided to be a smart boy."

"No sir."

"You decided to show a hick sheriff a thing or two."

"No sir."

"So you didn't get out of my way like everybody else because you think you're too smart to act like everybody else."

"No sir."

Dowd jabbed a porky finger hard into Tony's chest. "You just remember something, kid. I got everything in my favor. Everything. And you don't have squat. You know that?"

"Yes sir."

"And you better be damned careful what you do in this town, because you just managed to displease me one whole hell of a lot. And I sure ain't partial to being displeased."

Tony saw Steve in the shop doorway behind Dowd. Steve looked terrified.

"You understand me, kid?" Dowd said, poking Tony in the chest again.

"Yes sir."

Dowd scowled at all the people standing around gawking. "You folks get on about your business now. He isn't going to give you any more of a show, are you, kid?"

"No sir."

The people scattered like chickens in a barnyard.

"You made a dumb mistake, kid."

"Yes sir."

"You made an enemy when you didn't need to make an enemy."

"Yes sir."

Dowd looked Tony up and down. He didn't appear impressed by what he saw. "You're going to do something dumb while you're in town, kid, and I'm going to nail your ass to the wall. You know that?"

Tony said nothing.

"You know that?"

"I don't want to get into any trouble with you, sir."

Dowd snorted. "That's what you don't seem to understand, kid. You already are in trouble with me."

And with that, Dowd shoved Tony back against the shop again and started walking down the boardwalk, his spurs jangling and his hulking body making people scurry out of his way.

After a long moment, Steve came out of the shop. "He sure don't like you."

Tony looked after the sheriff. "He sure don't. But I don't give a damn about some hick sheriff."

"He said he was your enemy," Steve said.

Tony waved his hand dismissively. "He's some hayseed lawman is all."

But Tony knew better than that, of course. He knew he'd already made one mistake and that Sheriff Dowd would be begging him to make a second one.

Mr. Bruce Laymon, president of the area's largest bank, was enjoying himself. Laymon was happily married, so it wasn't other women that gave him pleasure. Nor was it liquor; Mr. Bruce Laymon was a teetotaler. Nor was the source of his pleasure a good cigar; his lip broke out whenever he put tobacco to his mouth.

No, what gave Mr. Bruce Laymon pleasure was watching important people squirm before him.

As now.

Here sat Mr. Carmody, one of the most arrogant people Laymon had ever known, sitting across the desk, virtually pleading for a loan.

Over the past two years, despite what most of the town thought, Mr. Carmody's investments had gone bad. Mr. Carmody was, for all practical purposes, broke.

The gray afternoon cast long shadows in the dark mahogany-paneled office. Only the forest-green silk shade of the kerosene lamp lent the room any color.

Laymon knew how difficult this was for Carmody, which only made Laymon enjoy it all the more.

"It's not just that we're business associates," Carmody said. "Hell, Bruce, we're friends."

Laymon almost winced at the word. Friends? Laymon had a bad limp from a boyhood riding accident. At parties—when Laymon was absent, of course—Carmody loved to do an imitation of how jerkily Laymon walked down a street. One night Laymon had seen this for himself, as he'd stood on a snowy walk and looked in at all the comfortable people inside, laughing at him in absentia.

Is that how friends treat each other? Bruce Laymon wanted to ask. God, I hope I have better friends than you, Carmody. I sure hope I do.

"I know things will turn back my way," Carmody said, the pleading tone in his voice once again.

"One would think so," Laymon said, purposefully trying to sound stuffy so that Carmody would get all the more irritated. "And one would hope so."

"I need five thousand is all, Bruce. Five thousand to tide me over the winter."

"That seems like a lot of money—for living expenses, I mean."

Carmody shrugged. "Well, the Christmas party alone will probably be five hundred."

My God, here sat a man on the verge of bankruptcy who was willing to make no sacrifices in his lifestyle whatsoever.

A Christmas party.

When the bastard couldn't afford a plug of tobacco.

"I'm afraid you'll have to forget about your Christmas party for this year anyway."

"Forget it?"

"You just can't afford it."

"But then everybody will know."

"Will know?"

"Of course. If I don't have my Christmas party then everybody will know what kind of shape I'm in financially."

Quite seriously, Laymon said, "Maybe that would be better."

"Better?"

"For you. For everybody. To know the truth. They might even come to your aid."

"Charity," Carmody said.

"Charity?"

"Hell yes, charity. Because that's exactly what it would be. Clucking around me and saying poor, stupid Carmody. He couldn't hold on to his fortune."

"What choice do you have?"

Carmody looked straight at him. "You could give me a loan."

"You forget, I have a board of directors."

"Meaning what?"

"Meaning they have to pass on every loan. If I told them that I wanted to give you five thousand dollars, they'd want to know why, and then they'd ask what collateral you were putting up."

"They ask *me* for collateral?" The whole notion seemed to scandalize Carmody. "My God, I'm an important man in this town."

Used to be, Laymon thought.

And so many people are going to be happy when they learn that you aren't important any longer.

All the wives you seduced; even a few older daughters here and there. And never showing the least interest in or sympathy for the decent people in this town.

Oh, you're going to fall far and you're going to fall hard, and there's not going to be a single person who's going to really give a damn. Not in their hearts, anyway.

"I can't do it," said Laymon out loud.

"I can't believe I'm sitting here listening to this. I'm only asking for five thousand dollars."

"I—" He shook his head. "I can make you a personal loan of two thousand, if that would help."

Laymon could see that the man's first impulse was to curse and turn down the loan. But Laymon knew just how desperate Carmody really was.

He couldn't afford to curse and turn down the loan.

Quietly, in barely a whisper, he asked, "When could I have the money?"

Laymon noted that he didn't smile or say thanks.

He was accepting charity and he knew it.

"I can put the money in your account now, if you'd like it."

"All right."

Laymon prepared himself to put the knife in one final time. "But I'll have to hold back two hundred and twenty dollars."

"Two hundred and twenty. But why?"

"Interest payment on the loan you made a year ago."

"Interest pay . . ." Carmody looked confused. He was one of those men who borrowed money in the belief that he would somehow never have to pay it back. He'd inherit a gold mine, or the man who loaned him the money would die in a fire and the debt would be canceled. A fantasy such as a small boy would have. But then Laymon considered all men who couldn't properly handle their finances to be small boys.

Carmody stood up. He was going to leave without saying so much as good-bye. Accepting the money had humiliated him beyond words.

Laymon let him get to the door, then he said, "I saw an old friend of yours on the street this morning."

Carmody looked preoccupied, disinterested. "Old friend?"

"Yes. Jenna."

At the name, Carmody's head snapped up. "Jenna?"

"Yes," Laymon said. "I was wondering if you remembered her."

Laymon thought, But then it's unlikely you'd forget raping a nine-year-old girl, isn't it?

"My God," Carmody said, suddenly looking and sounding like a very old man. "My God."

And then he was gone.

CHAPTER

★5★

They didn't look like the kind of men she would or should be hanging around with.

On his way back to Clifton's house, Matt saw Jenna standing on a corner talking with two hard cases. Even given the fact that Jenna had to scramble pretty hard to survive as an actress and probably had to hang out with some unsavory characters every once in a while, these men still looked hard and tough.

One of them was tall and almost pretty; he would have looked slick, except for the beard stubble and the wrinkled clothes. The other was pudgy and rumpled and sad; yet there was a definite air of violence about him too, like the hobos he sometimes saw riding the rails.

What was she doing with men like these?

This troubled Matt. The young woman had clearly come back to Templar to settle her score with the man who had raped her. Had she, for some reason, turned to men like these to help her?

He stood there on the corner, big wet snowflakes falling steadily now from the gray sky, women in heavy winter coats hurrying by as they did their shopping, and wondered if he shouldn't have a talk with Jenna to keep her from doing anything foolish.

But for now all he could do was stand there and watch the three of them walk away toward a cafe a few doors down the boardwalk.

Matt had a bad feeling about these men. A very bad feeling.

He gave her the scarf right away.

They'd barely sat down before Steve whipped out the small package in fancy wrapping paper and handed it over to her.

Predictably, Tony looked bored, even irritated by this. Clearly his attitude was that there were things to talk about. Why should they be wasting their time on things like this?

But he sat in the little booth in the little greasy cafe and let them go through their stupid little gift-giving.

Jenna liked it right away.

She lifted the wool scarf from its wrapping paper, held it up to the light, and said, "It's beautiful, Steve."

"I knew you'd like it." He blushed. He always did whenever he tried to express his feelings for her. She looked at Tony. She wished he'd show her half the consideration Steve did.

She put the scarf on and threw it festively around her neck.

"You sure do look pretty."

"Thank you, Steve." She looked at Tony again and smiled gently. "How about you?"

"Me?"

"Do you think I look pretty?"

"Oh. Yeah."

She tried to keep the hurt from her gaze. Tony hated emotions, like hurt and love and sentiment. He considered them awkward. He considered them useless. Her father had been like that, and sometimes she wished she didn't love Tony at all.

"We done with the partying now?" Tony said, glaring over at Steve.

Steve made a big thing of staring at the table. He didn't want to make Tony any angrier.

"He was just being nice," Jenna said.

"He can be nice some other time. We've got business to talk about. We didn't ride no thousand miles so Steve could buy you some scarf."

The harshness in his voice made both Jenna and Steve nervous. They dreaded Tony losing his temper. He had an incredible, unyielding temper. It took him forever to cool down. There was no way they wanted him to lose it now.

"This Carmody," Tony began.

"Yes," Jenna said.

"How much you think he's got in his house?"

"As I said in my letter, I don't know exactly how much, but I know he's a rich man and that he keeps a lot of it in a wall safe in his house."

Tony wouldn't come see her; he hadn't for months. She'd needed some ploy to lure him. So she'd told him about Carmody. She'd take care of two things this way: She'd keep Tony close *and* she'd get to extract some kind of vengeance from Carmody.

"How are you planning for us to get in there?" Tony asked.

"I'll go up to the door."

"And say what?"

"Just say that I was in town and that I wanted to talk to him."

"What makes you think he'll let you in."

"You remember what I told you," Jenna said.

And once more Tony looked uncomfortable, as if

Jenna would start sobbing again the way she had the night she'd told him all about being raped at so young an age by a proper and respected citizen like Carmody.

"So he lets you in. Then what?"

"Then I somehow manage to get to the back door and unlatch it so you can sneak in."

Steve said, "You're really smart, Jenna. You've got everything figured out."

"She doesn't have shit figured out," Tony said. "Not shit."

Jenna felt her cheeks grow red and hot and felt a terrible knot in her stomach. "What's wrong with the plan?"

"Everything."

"Could you be a little more specific?" she said, allowing herself the luxury of sarcasm.

Tony shook his head. "There's no guarantee you'll ever get to the back door."

"Why not?"

"Because he may not even let you inside to get to the back door."

"He'll let me in."

"Don't be too sure."

"Then what do you suggest?"

Tony said, "We go in right behind you at the front door."

"How do you do that?"

"We hide in the shadows when you go up to the door. While you're talking, with the door open, we put our guns on him and invite ourselves in."

At the mention of guns, Jenna said, "You remember our agreement."

"No violence," Steve said, sounding like a kid repeating a line a teacher had said.

"That's right," Jenna said.

Tony shrugged. "You can't ever rule it out."

"I can," Jenna said. "I just want to rob him—and then say a few things I've been wanting to say for a long time—and then we're on our way out of town."

"I just hope he's got as much money as you say," Tony said.

"Don't worry. He does."

Steve asked, "Can she put her scarf on again, Tony?"

"For shit's sake," Tony said.

"Just for a minute," Steve said.

Jenna smiled. "I'm glad somebody around here thinks I'm pretty."

"You're not pretty, Jenna. You're beautiful."

"Thank you, Steve."

"So will you put it on?"

Tony glowered as Jenna wrapped the scarf around her neck.

"Ain't she beautiful?" Steve asked Tony.

"Yeah. Beautiful."

Steve said, "I wish I had a picture of you like that, Jenna."

Tony said, "Seven would be a good time. It'll be full dark by then, and there won't be a lot of people walking around on the street."

"I wish you didn't have to bring guns," Jenna said. "I know you do, but . . ." She shook her head. "But don't use them. Promise me."

"I know what I'm doing," Tony said.

Jenna looked at him. Sometimes she wondered why she loved him at all. "I sure hope so. I sure do, Tony."

Matt had started to walk back to Clifton's house when he decided to find out what he could about the two men Jenna had been talking to.

He went to three different hotels, describing the men

to the desk clerks but getting no answers. No such men were registered.

He then tried both livery stables and got lucky in the second one. The Indian who worked there said that the men had left their horses off this morning. He had no idea where they could be found at the moment.

Matt started looking around town for Jenna. The third place he looked was the cafe he'd seen them enter. He saw them through the window. They were at a table, talking. He went across the street, smoked his pipe, and waited for them to come out.

The men looked just as bad as before.

He was still worried that Jenna might be getting herself into trouble. She was a bitter young woman.

By the time the trio came out half an hour later, Matt's cheeks were so cold they were numb. The snow had continued falling steadily, so that the top of Matt's flat-brimmed black hat and his shoulders and boots were covered with the stuff.

The two men and Jenna stood in front of the cafe, talking for a while. Once or twice Jenna glanced across the street to the doorway where Matt was leaning, but she didn't seem to recognize him.

Finally the men started away. One of them said something to her and then smiled. Jenna very dramatically threw the red woolen scarf around her neck. Both she and the one man laughed heartily about this.

Then the men were gone down the boardwalk, vanishing into the crowd.

Matt went across the street to join Jenna.

She was walking along briskly, about to enter her hotel, when he caught up with her.

"Afternoon."

She looked almost startled to see him. "Why, Mr. Ramsey."

He smiled. "I hoped I'd be 'Matt' by now."

She smiled too. " 'Matt' then."

"You like the hotel?"

"It's all right."

People came in and out, swirling around them.

"I guess I don't know how to say this," Matt began.

"You look awfully serious," she said, obviously trying to sound lighthearted.

"Nervous would be more like it."

"Nervous? Goodness, I hope it's not me."

He cleared his throat. He didn't believe in imposing himself in other people's business. But in this case . . .

"I just happened to be walking down the street a while ago."

"Yes."

"And I saw you."

She studied him. "Go on, Matt."

"I saw you with two men."

"Oh." The playful tone was entirely gone from her voice now.

"They weren't the sort of men I'd expect a nice young woman like you to be associated with."

She smiled sadly. "They are pretty rough looking, aren't they? Especially Tony. Handsome as he is, he can look pretty scary."

"I just hope . . ." He stopped and shook his head.

"You just hope what, Matt?"

"I just hope you're not planning anything foolish."

She dropped her gaze to her small gloved hands. "I don't see where what I do is any of your business."

"To be honest, Jenna, neither do I. I'm real uncomfortable talking to you about this because you're a grown woman and you can make your own decisions. It's just that sometimes all of us . . ."

"All of us what, Matt?"

"All of us make bad decisions."

She looked up at Matt again. The anger had returned to her gaze. "He raped me when I was nine years old."

"I know."

"And not one person in this town would do anything about it."

"I know that too."

"So don't you think I've got some due coming?"

Matt said, "You've got more friends in this town than you realize."

"Oh?"

He told her how Deputy Wisdom was going to confront the subject of Jenna's rape and how it'd been covered up all these years.

"Wisdom?" she said. "He's just a boy."

"He's your age."

"But up against Dowd?" She shook her head. "I appreciate what the doctor's trying to do, but I don't think it's going to help much."

"Those men," Matt said.

"What about them, Matt?"

"I . . . wish—"

She sighed and then reached out and put her hand on his. "You know something?"

"What?"

"I'm really touched by this."

Matt didn't know what to say.

"But believe it or not, Matt, those two men are friends of mine. Good friends."

"I see."

"And if they're bad, then I'm bad too. They won't do anything I don't tell them to."

He stared at her again. "Why don't you give Wisdom a little time?"

"Because I've given this town ten years to do what's

right. Can't you see that, Matt?"

"I suppose. But—"

"Now you go see your friend the doctor. And tell him that I appreciate all his good thoughts and his letter and everything else. And tell him not to worry about me. Tell him that I know what I'm doing and that I can handle it all very well by myself. Will you please give him that message?"

"All right."

She laughed. "You look like a sad little animal."

"Sometimes that's how I feel."

"Things are going to be all right, Matt. I promise."

But she couldn't get the icy rage from her voice nor her eyes.

He didn't know what she was planning, but he was sure that it wasn't anything he was going to like.

CHAPTER

★6★

Wisdom waited till Sheriff Dowd got all fixed up in his office before going in and bothering him.

Dowd liked to tell everybody that he kept his door closed because he was going through all the papers and documents from the preceding day.

Everybody knew better. Dowd liked to lock himself into his office, put his big booted feet on the desk, pick up a copy of the local paper, and then start munching on the candy that filled the bottom left-hand drawer of his desk.

Wisdom was a past master at irritating the sheriff.

He'd always wait till Dowd's chair made that squawking noise as Dowd leaned back, and then wait till Dowd sighed in that contented way of his, and then Wisdom would knock.

Dowd always started out by swearing under his breath.

Today was no different. He called the knocker a sonofabitch and then said, "What is it?"

"I need to talk to you."

"Wisdom?"

"Yes sir."

"Can't it wait?"

"Pretty important, Sheriff."

Under his breath Dowd said, "Shit." Then aloud: "I'm pretty damned busy with these papers. Couldn't you hold on for a while?"

"Like to, but afraid I can't."

Dowd said, "Shit!" under his breath again.

Then he heaved himself up from the chair—after all, there was a lot of man there to heave—and jangled over to the door, getting in a few more swear words as he moved.

He opened the door, and there stood Wisdom.

"What is it, Wisdom?"

"Letter."

"What letter?"

"This letter." He waggled the white envelope at him.

"You think I'm going to play some kind of goddamn guessing game with you, Wisdom? Give me that fucking letter right now."

"Probably I'd better read it to you, sir."

"Who's the goddamn sheriff here, Wisdom, me or you, huh?"

"You are, sir. But this letter may be introduced as evidence some day."

"Evidence? In what? What the hell are you talking about?"

"Evidence against you for covering up a crime."

"Just what the hell're you talkin' about?" Dowd said.

Wisdom fanned the letter at him again. "As you know, Doc Ruark is dyin'."

"Yeah. So what?"

"Well, he decided to remind this town of the truth."

"What truth?"

Wisdom paused and looked at the short, chubby, red-faced man. "The truth about Jenna Fairbain."

Dowd didn't have to say anything. His reaction was

all in his eyes. He managed to look angry and scared at the same time.

"Just what the hell kind of game are you playin' here, Wisdom?"

"I want Carmody arrested and I want this town to apologize to Jenna."

Dowd surprised him by laughing—a deep, true belly laugh. And he certainly had the belly for it. "And then what, Wisdom? Everybody go to a prayer meetin' and join hands and praise the Lord for all He give us?"

Dowd was still laughing when Wisdom quietly said, "He should go to prison."

"Carmody?"

"Yep." Wisdom didn't take his eyes off Dowd now. "And you."

"What the hell should I go to prison for?"

"For covering up a rape."

"Listen, you stupid young hayseed sonofabitch, I was wearing a badge before you wiggled out of your mama's pussy. And don't you forget it."

"You're going to be arrested, Dowd. And I'm going to see to it. And I'm going to do it right after I arrest Carmody."

Dowd glared at him. "He may look like a dandy, sonny boy, but he's one mean sonofabitch. As you're about to find out."

Wisdom said, "You could always join me, Dowd."

"No thanks."

"Doing your duty even after all these years is better than not doing it at all."

Dowd smirked. "I want to see what you look like when Carmody gets done with you."

"He won't do much when I present him with a warrant."

"And just where are you goin' to get a warrant?"

"From Judge Osgood."

Dowd snorted. "You really are dumb. You think Judge Osgood is really goin' to give you a warrant?"

"After I show him the letter."

"He'll be afraid to cross me," the sheriff said.

"We'll see, Sheriff," Wisdom said. "We'll see."

And with that, he turned and walked out of the office.

"Pain," Winona said.

"Worse?"

"A lot worse."

"I'm sorry."

"He's resting, but he's not asleep. He'd be glad to see you."

Matt wasn't sure he knew what to say to his old friend. All the reassuring cliches meant nothing at a time like this. Obviously the man was dying. Obviously he was in almost intolerable pain.

Winona led the way into the room, pulling back the drapes as she went in.

Midafternoon shadows hid in the corners, about to leap with coming night.

Clifton looked paler and even more haggard than he had that morning.

His eyes turned in Matt's direction, but for a long and terrible moment there seemed to be no recognition in them whatsoever.

"Howdy," Matt said.

And finally Clifton spoke. "I'm sorry you have to see me like this, Matt."

"Oh hell, Clifton. We're friends."

"It's still spooky, and I know it. People think docs get used to seeing people die. But I'll tell you a little secret: We never get used to it at all. Oh, we pretend we do for the sake of the loved ones standing around—

they don't like us when we're not strong and wise and all knowing—but we don't know any more about the hereafter than a layman does."

Matt sat down next to the bed. "I delivered your letter to Wisdom."

"What'd he say?"

"He said he'd do it."

Pure glee showed on the dying man's face. "I knew he was a good man."

"Dowd isn't going to be very happy."

"And neither is Carmody. Or Judge Osgood."

And then Clifton fell to coughing.

Matt stared down at his fists, not knowing what else to do.

When Clifton stopped coughing, he said, "You know what I'm praying for?"

"What?"

"That I can live just long enough to see this town make it right with Jenna."

Matt smiled. "With Wisdom working on it, I'd say you'll be sure to see it. If she keeps her head."

"Meaning what, Matt?"

Matt told him about Tony and Steve.

"You think they've got something planned?"

"I don't know. But they sure look like hardcases."

Clifton frowned. "I can't say that I blame her. All these years when nobody made any trouble about what happened to her." He looked at Matt directly. "Including me."

"You've done all you could."

"I could've done more and I know it."

"No sense blaming yourself, Clifton. You had to live here. You couldn't get involved any more than you already had."

Clifton sank back into his pillow. He looked almost

ghostly, his eyes shining with sickness, his thin lips parched and white. "I just hope she doesn't do anything crazy. The law's going to help her now. With Wisdom, I mean."

"I'm going to go have a talk with those two men myself."

Clifton looked at him sharply. "No sense you getting in any trouble, Matt. If these two are the hardcases you say they are—"

"I'll be fine, Clifton. Don't worry about me."

Clifton laughed then. "I guess I should remember what you did to those two Yankees in that saloon after the war."

Matt smiled. "Good thing I'd had a lot of whiskey or I'd never have done it."

"Never thought I'd see one man whip two others."

"Just got lucky."

Clifton stared at him. There were tears in the man's eyes now. "You're a good friend, Matt. Without you and Winona—"

"You just lay back and relax, my friend."

Clifton did what Matt said. But just before closing his eyes and falling asleep, he said, "I sure hope we can help Jenna."

"I sure hope so too. Clifton. I sure hope so too."

Judge Fenton Osgood had a spread on the northern edge of town. Ranch hands helped him raise beef cattle that were then loaded onto trains and shipped to Omaha, which paid top dollar for beeves in those days.

Like many frontier judges, Osgood had little legal training as such. But he did have a real interest in the law and he certainly had good political connections in the governor's mansion, so getting a judgeship hadn't been all that difficult. The consensus among educated lawyers was that Osgood was a pretty good judge if he didn't have a personal stake in the verdict. God help you, though, if you tried to bring justice down on Osgood or one of his cronies. He'd once tried to get a lawyer disbarred for merely bringing suit against an Osgood cousin in a civil matter.

So as he rode out to Osgood's spread, Deputy Wisdom didn't feel an abundance of hope. He figured that the judge would do pretty much what Sheriff Dowd had predicted: laugh and then throw him out.

The paint Wisdom rode kept sneezing at the snow-flakes. Wisdom huddled inside his sheep-lined jacket and tilted his head down against the raw wind.

Most of the cattle were in a metal lean-to when Wisdom drew abreast of the road leading to the large brick ranch house.

Afternoon was beginning to gray into dusk so everything looked dirty: the livestock pens that smelled sweetly of shit despite the cold, the outbuildings built of raw lumber, and the dozen or so pigs that squatted in their own frozen feces over by the grain silo.

Wisdom ground-tied his paint and then went up to the door.

A stooped, aged Mexican man answered. This was Lupe. It was said that the judge treated him terribly, but if that were the case Lupe sure didn't seem to mind. He was as loyal as a brother to the judge.

"Yes, Señor Wisdom?"

"I'd like to see the judge, Lupe."

"He is napping."

"Afraid I'll have to ask you to wake him."

The old man tilted his graying head toward Wisdom. "Do you know what happens if I wake the judge from his nap?"

Wisdom smiled. "I'll take responsibility, Lupe. I promise."

Wisdom caught a glimpse of the house inside. A vast stone fireplace crackled and roared with a blazing fire. It looked most inviting on a cold bleak afternoon such as this one.

"We shouldn't talk much longer," Lupe said. "The judge wakes easily."

"Lupe, I really need to—"

But before Wisdom could finish his sentence, an authoritative male voice shouted, "Who the hell woke me up, Lupe?"

Lupe gulped and made a quick sign of the cross. He then slammed the door in Wisdom's face.

Wisdom just stood there.

Approximately half a minute passed.

Suddenly the door was flung open. A small man of no more than five-five stood there. He was shaggy, with a huge walrus mustache and the meanest blue eyes Wisdom had ever seen. He wore a rawhide shirt decorated with Indian beads and matching rawhide pants. In his right hand he carried a huge Frontier Colt.

"What the hell do you want, Wisdom?" Judge Osgood boomed.

And Wisdom, who'd felt so cocksure, so self-confident, even so belligerent just a few moments before, swallowed hard just as Lupe had and said, "I just need a few minutes of your time, Your Honor."

He realized how young and vulnerable he sounded, and he cursed himself for it.

"For what?"

Wisdom gulped again. It had all seemed so easy. He'd just ride out here, demand a warrant, and threaten to ride through two counties and get another judge to give him a warrant if Osgood here didn't come through.

But now that he was actually standing in front of the man . . .

Now that the man was actually glaring at him and shouting in his face . . .

"I need a warrant because I want to arrest Sheriff Dowd and Mr. Carmody and—"

"My *friends* Sheriff Dowd and Mr. Carmody?"

"Yes sir."

The judge looked at Wisdom as if the young deputy had lost his mind.

Then the judge raised the Frontier Colt and pointed it right at Wisdom's face.

"Get in here," the judge said.

"Sir?"

"I said get in here. I don't know about you, but I'm freezing my ass off."

"Yes sir."

He leveled the Colt directly at Wisdom's heart now. "So get your ass in here right now."

"Yes sir."

And with that, Wisdom went inside the fancy ranch house.

Judge Osgood thunderously slammed the door behind him.

Wisdom felt like an animal that had just gotten its foot caught in a steel trap.

Around three that afternoon, Tony told Steve that he wanted to go for a walk alone and that he'd meet him back at the tavern in half an hour. Steve was used to Tony acting this way. Sometimes he got the feeling that Tony just couldn't stand being around him and needed to get away. Steve never said anything, never complained. He always did what Tony told him, otherwise Tony would leave him; and if Tony left him, what the hell would Steve do? Steve knew he wasn't a genius. He needed a Tony to do his thinking for him. So all Steve said when Tony downed the last of his beer was "Okay, Tony, see you in a little while."

Steve drifted over to the pool table to watch two local hustlers try to impress each other and all the onlookers, and Tony went out the door.

Whatever small buzz he'd been getting from the beer evaporated in the cold air.

Tony liked the feeling of raw power the cold air gave him.

He went directly to the livery stable and found the Indian who worked there.

As the man was pitching hay, Tony went up to him and said, "Want to talk to you a minute, chief."

He called all Indians "chief." Steve was convinced that this was a very funny joke.

The Indian quit baling and looked at Tony. He said nothing; he just waited for Tony to continue.

"I want my horse fed and rubbed down and saddled and ready to go at nine tonight." He then gave the Indian a double eagle. "This should take care of it."

"Your friend brought a horse too."

"I don't want his horse ready."

The Indian looked at Tony suspiciously. Tony was never subtle. Obviously the Indian knew right away that something was wrong here.

"You don't want his horse ready?"

"No. In fact I want you to tell him that his horse took sick."

The Indian just looked at him.

Tony handed over another gold double eagle.

"Can you do that for me, chief?"

The Indian looked at the money in the palm of his hand.

"So he isn't your friend?"

"Who?"

"The other man with the horse."

Tony shrugged. "Seems to me that's sort of my business, chief. All you have to remember is that I'll be here at nine on the dot. You understand?"

The Indian nodded.

Tony left and went back out into the dying day. His plan was simple enough. There would be three dead bodies at the Carmody place that night: Carmody, Steve, and Jenna. Easy enough to make it look as though there'd been a shootout and Carmody had killed them and died himself in the process.

Tony would have the loot and would be far, far away.

And he would be shut of both Jenna and Steve, two people who weighed on him like a terrible obligation.

As he walked now, he started to whistle. He hadn't whistled in a long time.

CHAPTER

★7★

Matt stood on the outside of the batwing doors, looking inside the saloon.

The place was mostly used for gambling of various kinds—everything from poker to faro—which meant that it was also a popular place for freeloaders. A ham sandwich was only a nickel and a shell of beer three cents. A man could play a cheap game of blackjack and pretend to be thinking over some more gambling, then eat a hell of a lot of food in the process.

He didn't see the men he was looking for, but then the saloon, as dusk drew closer, was crowded. The professional girls, who usually came on around three when the largest of the local factories was changing shift, had already started working, passing among the tables and making old farts wish they were young again and making young farts wish they didn't have such responsibilities as wives and pink-cheeked little babies.

He decided to go inside and look around anyway.

A player piano was booming out a popular tune called "Buffalo Gal," while a geezer in arm garters and a muley sat next to the player on a stool, strumming his ass off on a banjo. The only customer who seemed to be paying any attention was an old sourdough who looked as if he were on the verge of going over there and putting the banjo up a narrow passage in the musician's anatomy.

The floor was a mess of snow and mud. A pathetic, scraggly Christmas tree sat at one end of the bar. Instead of an angel sitting on top, a wag had put a naked doll there, and somebody with a pen had drawn in nipples on the doll's breasts. This place was just chock full of the real Christmas spirit.

Matt had himself a shell, and when he got about halfway through with it, he glanced in the mirror behind the bar and saw the two of them walk in.

Tony and Steve, Jenna had called them.

Seen up close, Matt's initial impression of the two was confirmed. The dark one looked smart and cunning, the blond one looked thick and dumb.

They went to the opposite end of the bar and got themselves schooners. One of the saloon girls came up and flirted briefly with Tony and he flirted back—as if the girl might be brokenhearted if he didn't favor her with his attention—but then he told her to get away from them and he went back to talking quietly with Steve.

Matt went over to them.

"Excuse me," he said.

Tony swung around and looked at Matt as if he were something a dog had just shit on the ground.

"You want something?"

"I'd like to talk to you."

"Oh yeah?"

"Yeah."

Tony looked at Steve and winked. Then he looked back at Matt. "You law?"

"Nope."

"You mayor?"

"Nope."

He grinned. "You got much money?"

"Uh-uh."

Tony winked at Steve again and looked once more at Matt. "Then why the hell should I talk to you?"

"Because I think you can help me with a friend of mine."

"Oh yeah?"

"Yeah."

"And just who would this friend be?"

"Her name is Jenna."

The joshing left Tony's eyes. This time when he glanced over at Steve there was a mixture of curiosity and anxiety in his eyes.

"What about Jenna?" he said to Matt.

"She's a nice girl."

"So?"

"So I want her to stay a nice girl."

"Meaning what, exactly?"

"Meaning I don't want her to get mixed up in anything she'll regret."

Tony took out a cigar, sniffed it, bit off the end, spat the end on the floor, and then put the cigar in his mouth.

Steve lit it for him.

Matt was surprised that Steve would want to be a toady for a greaseball like Tony. But then Matt was also surprised that a good girl like Jenna would want to have anything to do with Tony either.

"Jenna's never mentioned you," Tony said.

"I met her on the stage coming in."

"Isn't that cozy?"

"She told me what happened here when she was nine. I get the feeling that she's got something planned and I want to stop it. And if you care for Jenna at all, you won't let her go through with it."

Tony looked at him. "You must be a preacher."

"Far from it."

"Cause that's what you sound like." Tony glanced at Steve and grinned. His eyes came back to Matt's. "Yes sir, that's just what you sound like."

Matt saw Tony's right hand drop closer to the handle of his Colt.

Matt's own hand fell to his .44.

"I don't have much patience with punks," Matt said. "You reach for that Colt of yours and I'm going to put two bullets right in your heart."

"You tryin' to scare me?"

"Just trying to make you be reasonable."

"Come on, Tony," Steve said. "He means it."

"You keep out of this, asshole, you understand?" He glared at Steve. Steve shrunk into himself.

Tony now glared at Matt. "So you're a tough guy, huh?"

"Tougher than you are, anyway," Matt said.

Tony's hand drifted away from his gun.

"I just wanted to warn you about Jenna," Matt said.

"Warn me?"

Now it was Matt's turn to glare. "If she does anything foolish, I'm going to hold you two punks responsible. You understand?"

Steve gulped, obviously afraid.

Tony still tried to look tough, but Matt's words had taken their toll. There was now a growing apprehension in the dark gaze.

Matt said, "I just wanted you to know that."

Then he turned and stalked out of the saloon.

Sheriff Dowd wasn't a man used to hurrying: He had deputies to do that for him.

But now he had no choice but to hurry.

He moved through the late afternoon gloom of the town, too busy to appreciate any of the Christmas candles glowing prettily in the front windows of stores and private homes alike.

He walked to the edge of town, to where Carmody's rambling Victorian home sat imposingly even in the darkness.

Only one downstairs light burned.

Dowd went to the front door and knocked.

When Carmody finally appeared, he wore a red smoking jacket and carried a fancy goblet half filled with wine that was no doubt expensive.

He wouldn't have anything like this in prison, Dowd thought.

Dowd didn't wait to be invited in.

He went inside, tracking mud all the way into the living room.

Carmody slammed the door behind him.

"What the hell do you think you're doing?"

"A favor," Dowd said. "I'm doing you a favor. That's what."

"Tracking mud across my Persian rug is a favor?"

"Fuck your Persian rug, Carmody."

"Why did you break in here like this?"

"Because we're about to get served arrest warrants."

"What the hell are you talking about?"

Dowd told him.

"She's pressing charges after all this time?"

"She isn't," Dowd said. "Doc Ruark is."

"Why the hell would he care about somebody like Jenna?"

"You know Ruark. A born do-gooder if there ever was one."

Carmody stared reflectively into his glass of wine. "What happens next?"

"Wisdom takes over this town."

"You're crazy."

"Think about it. That's what he's wanted to do ever since I made the mistake of hiring him as my deputy. Clean it up. Throw in with the reformers. And if he succeeds in arresting you and me—"

Carmody hurled his wineglass into the fireplace. "Well, he's not going to succeed, I can tell you that."

And with that he left the room, to appear a minute later without his fancy smoking jacket and carrying a carbine. "You say he's out at Judge Osgood's?"

"Right."

"Well, I can go out to Judge Osgood's too."

"You sure you want to do this, Carmody?"

But of course that's exactly what Dowd wanted him to do.

"You're damned right it is," Carmody said.

"Come to my office when you're done."

Carmody looked at the muddy footprints across his living room. He smirked at Dowd. "Yes, and I'll be sure to track some mud in when I come."

Dowd, the fat slob that he was, didn't laugh.

Jenna felt drained and she didn't know why.

She'd come back to her room in the late afternoon and was napping when a knock came at her door.

At first she felt disoriented, the way she usually did when she awakened. Who was she? Where was she? What was this fear she felt?

But then she heard a familiar voice on the other side of the door.

She got up, slipped into her dress, brushed at her hair with her fingers, went over and lit the kerosene lamp on the bureau, and then went to the door.

He looked bigger and more pathetic than usual, standing in the doorway. He also looked scared. "You promise not to tell?"

"Tell what, Steve?"

"Tell Tony I come over here."

"Is everything all right?"

"I gotta tell you somethin'."

"All right."

"But you promise?"

"Yes, I promise."

And with that she stood back so Steve could come inside and take a seat on the straight-backed chair by the bureau.

On the roof slanting away from the window, Jenna could see that snow was already piling heavily. Outside it must be pretty bad.

She went and sat on the edge of the bed and looked at Steve. Sometimes he got excited this way. At these times he was like a young child who'd been spooked by imaginary monsters in the dark.

"What's wrong, Steve?"

"I don't think we should do this."

"You mean go over to Carmody's tonight?"

"Uh-huh."

"Why not?"

"Because I had one of them dreams."

"One of what dreams?"

"You know. How I dream something and it comes true."

"Oh. Right."

Sometimes Steve had dreams—warnings, really—and they came true. Small things, though, like when a creek would overrun and they'd get stuck on the wrong side, or when Jenna would lose her purse and then be broke.

"The other night I had a dream about tonight."

"What about it?"

"I seen you shot."

Despite her better judgment, Jenna felt her stomach tense. "Who shot me?"

"I don't know."

She didn't want to ask this next question, but she did anyway. Her voice sounded eerie in the flickering light of the kerosene lantern, in the dark shadows of the winter night. "Did I die?"

"I don't know that either."

"You just saw me . . . shot?"

"Yeah . . . on the floor. Blood all over your shoulder and your arm."

She shuddered.

"I don't think we should go tonight, Jenna."

"Did you tell this to Tony?"

"You know him. He'd just laugh, is all."

"Where is he now?"

"Supper. I snuck off."

She thought of how long she'd hated Carmody. "I really wanted to go there tonight."

"I know."

"You can't know how much I hate this man."

"I don't want to see you get hurt, is all."

"I'm sure I'll be all right, Steve."

Steve shrugged and stood up. "I just wanted to tell you."

She got up and went over to him. She kissed him tenderly on the cheek.

He dropped his gaze, embarrassed.

"I appreciate your friendship, Steve."

He couldn't move. She'd never kissed him before. He had absolutely no idea what to do.

"But don't worry. Things'll work out. You'll see."

She led him to the door and back out into the hallway.

He made small, sad sounds as he disappeared down the stairs.

She went back and sat down on the edge of the bed and looked out the window.

Steve's dream . . .

But no, she dismissed it from her mind.

She'd waited too long for anything to get in the way of tonight.

Anything.

She was going to leave town a rich woman, and Carmody was going to find himself humiliated.

She lay down again and thought of how much fun tonight would be.

Wisdom sat on the edge of a large leather armchair and listened to Judge Osgood say "You got proof of what you say?"

"Right here." Wisdom waggled the envelope at him.

"Let me see it."

Wisdom got up and took the envelope over to the judge. They were in the den, in front of a small fireplace, surrounded by built-in bookcases stuffed with legal books and novels that ran to Sir Walter Scott and James Fenimore Cooper.

Wisdom went back to his chair and sat down.

The judge read the letter.

In fact, he read the letter twice.

When he finished with it the second time, he asked, "You got this from Doc Ruark?"

"From a man named Matt Ramsey. He got it from Doc Ruark."

"So you don't doubt that it's authentic."

"No, sir."

"Do you know this Jenna?"

"I know who she is, sir."

"And she's back in town now?"

"Yes, sir."

"You know where?"

"Staying at one of the hotels, I think."

The judge sat back in his leather armchair and studied the letter once more. "I don't have to tell you what this letter means for Templar."

"Sir?"

"It means the end of Templar as we know it. The power structure, at any rate."

"I guess so, sir."

"I'd have to give you warrants for Carmody and Dowd."

Wisdom sighed. "I'd be willing to serve them."

The judge smiled. "You wouldn't mind being sheriff, would you?"

"No, sir."

"In fact, it's fair to say that you would like to be sheriff, isn't it?"

Wisdom shrugged. "Guess so, sir."

The judge consulted the letter one more time. "You wouldn't have concocted this letter just so you could get Dowd out of the way, would you?"

Wisdom looked shocked.

The judge smiled again. "I didn't really think so, son. I just wanted to be sure."

He slid the letter back into the envelope, got up and crossed the room, and gave the letter back to Wisdom.

"You've got your warrants, son."

"Thank you, sir."

The judge looked down at Wisdom. "You realize that Dowd isn't going to go along easily?"

"I know that, sir."

"He's likely to get his other two deputies to try and kill you."

"Yes, sir."

"So you be careful."

"Yes, sir."

The judge glanced at the window. It had started snowing again. It felt snug and good to be inside at dinnertime when it was snowing and cold like this.

The judge turned back to Wisdom. "I knew that someday somebody would have nerve enough to stand up to Dowd and Carmody. And it's finally happened."

Wisdom grinned. "Maybe we'll have some real law and order in these parts now, instead of just cronyism."

The judge patted him on the back. "That's going to be up to you, son. That's going to be up to you."

The judge led Wisdom through the darkened house to the front door. Dinner smells came from the kitchen. Wisdom's mouth watered. He wanted to sit down in front of a warm stove and fill his young belly.

At the front door, the judge said, "This'll be a new era for Templar, son, and we owe it all to you."

Wisdom waved the letter at him. "And to Doc Ruark."

Wisdom shrugged into his sheep-lined coat and walked out to the hitching rail where his horse waited.

Darkness had already fallen. Snow still fell steadily.

He was putting one foot in the stirrup and one hand on the horn when the gunman opened fire.

Wisdom got hit with three shots. One got him in the shoulder, one got him in the neck, and one got him near the small of the back.

The force of the bullets spun him around completely, pitching Wisdom to the ground.

The judge, hearing the shots, burst from the front door and rushed over to Wisdom.

He cradled the young deputy's head in his arms and said, "Don't try to move, Wisdom. Lupe and I will get you inside."

The judge had no idea if Wisdom was still alert. Hell, there was probably even the chance that he was already dead.

Lupe ran from the house, carrying a blanket.

They covered the fallen deputy and then set about lifting him up by his arms and legs.

"Careful," the judge said.

And then the old man's head snapped up as he heard the sound of metal striking hard earth. The killer was riding away, swallowed up in the darkness.

"Careful," the judge said again as they carried Wisdom inside.

CHAPTER

★8★

Around seven, full dark now, Winona brought a tray of food into the bedroom where Matt sat talking with Clifton. They were recalling some of their adventures in the Civil War. Funny how, in the midst of unimaginable bloodshed, good memories could be made. They laughed gently about the Kentucky kid who'd always sing everybody to sleep at night, like a momma tucking in her loved ones; about the redheaded corporal who hated Yankees so much he'd stand straight up in the midst of battle to fire off his rounds; and about the small contingent of black soldiers who fought on the side of the Rebs despite becoming pariahs in their own community.

Winona stood in the doorway a long moment, listening to the two old friends laugh. She was grateful to Matt for coming. She hadn't seen her father enjoying himself this much in a long, sad time.

Dinner was roast beef, American fries, gravy, and green beans.

She served both men. Her father ate about what she'd expected—not much. But he obviously wanted Matt to eat and enjoy himself, so he went ahead and did some serious work on his meal, and meanwhile Matt, who had a good strong appetite, started cleaning up his plate.

Winona stayed and listened, then started asking her father to tell her again some of the stories he'd told her after the war.

Her father talked until the words exhausted him and he sank back into his pillow.

He had just started dozing off when there was a loud pounding on the front door—loud even above the icy, whistling wind.

Winona went to the door and saw Henry Evars, the newspaper editor, standing there. He looked half crazy about something.

"Wisdom," he said.

"What?"

"Wisdom," he repeated.

And then he came straight inside.

He was bundled up in a red wool cap with ear flaps and a bearskin coat that looked as if it weighed a hundred pounds.

He stood on the small throw rug and stamped snow off his feet.

By now Matt had come from the bedroom. He carried the dinner tray, having picked up all the dishes.

"You said Wisdom."

"Yes, Winona, I did."

"What about him?"

"Shot."

"What?" Matt said, coming closer.

"The way I understand it, he took a letter from Doc Ruark out to Judge Osgood's place so that he could get a warrant—and somebody shot him."

"Oh, God," Winona said, looking helplessly at Matt. "Where is he now?"

"Still at the judge's. But Osgood don't know what to do."

"Why not?" Matt said.

Evars, snow and ice covering his formidable gray mustache, said, "Ain't got no doc. Not with Doc Ruark down."

Matt shook his head. "Where's the closest one?"

"Fifty miles. Trail's End."

"You couldn't get there with this blizzard coming," Winona said.

Matt asked, "You have a buggy?"

"Sure. Why?"

"I'll need it," Matt said.

"What're you going to do?" Winona asked.

"Go get Wisdom. Bring him back here. Maybe your father would be strong enough to . . ."

She smiled. "And it would be good for him too, to doctor somebody."

"You may not be able to make it, mister," Evars said. "This blizzard."

"I'll need your best horse," Matt said. "That way I've got even odds, anyway."

Evars tugged his woolen mittens back on. "You know where the livery stable is?"

"Yep."

"Meet me there in fifteen minutes. I'll have everything ready to go." Then Evars looked at Winona. "You tell your father hello for me too."

"I'll do that."

Evars glanced at Matt once again. "Personally, son, I think you're taking a hell of a chance. This is the kind of storm people die in. But—well, I guess that's up to you."

Matt said, "I'll be all right."

Evars nodded to Winona and left.

Winona said, "You sure you want to do this, Matt?"

But Matt was already gathering up his heavy outer clothes for the trek ahead of him. "I'll be fine," he said.

"I sure hope you can save Wisdom," she said.

He smiled. "Do I detect more than a passing interest in that young man?"

She smiled back. "I've had a crush on him since I was eight years old."

"Does he know that?"

"He should by now. I used to follow him around like a love-sick calf."

Bundled up in his coat now, Matt gave her a hug. "I'll see that he gets back here all right."

And then he was gone.

Carmody sat by the fireplace, a snifter of brandy in his hand, trying to get warm.

The ride back from Judge Osgood's had been freezing and treacherous. About halfway his horse had developed snow blindness and started drifting away from the road. It took all of Carmody's might and concentration to keep the horse on the road.

The knock startled him.

Carmody got up, keeping his glass in his hand, and went to the front door.

There, almost lost in the blowing, drifting snow, he saw the chunky form of Sheriff Dowd.

Carmody opened the door.

Dowd said nothing. He just pushed himself inside.

"We have a problem," he said.

Once again he tracked mud and snow into the living room. He went over by the fireplace and began slapping his freezing hands together. "Sonofabitch, it's cold out there." Clearly he knew he was irritating Carmody by not talking about what had brought him here. But just as clearly he was enjoying himself.

"What the hell problem are you talking about?"

Dowd looked at him. In the firelight, his face looked grotesque. "You didn't kill Wisdom."

"What the hell are you talking about? Of course I did."

Dowd shook his head. The ice and snow on his mustache had just begun to melt. "You shot him up pretty bad, but you didn't kill him."

"Bullshit."

"Bullshit yourself."

"Where'd you hear this?"

"One of my deputies had to stop over to Doc Ruark's a little while ago. That Matt Ramsey feller went out to Judge Osgood's to bring Wisdom back so Doc Ruark can work on him."

"Doc Ruark? He's dying."

"But he's still got strength enough to take bullets out of somebody."

Carmody made a fist and slammed it into his other palm. "I thought for sure I killed him."

"You shot him up real good but he didn't die." Dowd clubbed his cold hands together again. "If we can kill Wisdom, we'll be all right."

"Why's that?"

"Because nobody else in town'll be willing to stand up to us. Wisdom's the only one."

Carmody shook his head. "I don't have any money left, Dowd. You should know that right now."

Dowd smiled at him. "You don't think that's a secret, do you? I've known you were broke for the past year." He slapped his hands together again. "But that isn't what matters now. Even if you don't have any money, you're not in prison. And if Wisdom lives, that's where you and

I'll both be: territorial prison for sure."

"What the hell do you have in mind?"

"Taking another pass at him," Dowd said.

"When?"

"Right now. When Ramsey's bringing him into town."

Carmody immediately saw the sense in that. "I guess that isn't a bad idea."

"Ramsey left an hour ago. With the snow bein' the way it is, that means he'll be back here in another hour, hour and a half. I figured you could wait for him at Raven's Rock and fire on him from there."

"Good idea."

"Just watch out for wolves."

Carmody shook his head, knowing Dowd wasn't kidding. Raven's Rock marked the beginning of miles of timber, land that was filled with wolves. Sudden changes in weather such as this one sometimes brought the animals down from the hills. Weather affected their moods. Normally peaceful animals who never attacked men, they were known to charge at men during times of great stress.

"Don't worry about that," Carmody said.

Dowd looked at the fire and shook his head. "I just started to get warm and now I've got to go back outside and get cold all over again."

Carmody laughed. "Life's a bitch, isn't it, Sheriff?"

And with that Dowd tracked more mud and snow across the floor on his way to the front door.

"Good luck," he said.

He jerked the door open and stepped out into the black, howling night.

Tony said, "It's that hick sheriff."

"What the hell's he doin' here?" Steve said.

"Don't know," Tony said.

They stood behind a thick stand of poplars directly across from Carmody's house.

Behind them, Jenna was huddled into her heavy cape and cowl.

To be heard, one had to yell above the roaring wind.

Sheriff Dowd came out on the porch, waved good-bye to Carmody, then set off down the snow-covered street toward the downtown area.

Carmody closed the door, taking away the long golden stream of light that had splashed across the front porch and out into the night.

Now the only illumination was Carmody's front window. Even with the drapes securely closed, they could see light around the edges of the window.

Warm, friendly light. The three of them had been standing out there for twenty minutes now, awaiting the right moment to approach Carmody's house.

Now was the right moment.

Soon they would be inside, getting warm and making themselves rich with all of Carmody's possessions.

And at last Jenna would have her vengeance.

At last.

"Let's go now," Tony said.

"You sure?" Steve said.

He was still afraid, and it showed. But then that was Steve's nature—to be afraid. Tony found him disgusting.

Jenna said, "I want your word, Tony. Your solemn word."

Tony grinned. "You got a Bible, I'll swear on it."

"You promised, Tony, you promised," Jenna said, her voice getting hoarse with all the shouting she had to do.

Wind and snow whipped at her face. Her nose and chin were absolutely numb.

"Say it, Tony," she said.

"Aw shit, Jenna, I already said it."

"Say it, or I won't go in there with you."

Tony said, "I promise not to hurt him." Then he looked at her and shook his head. "There, that make you feel any better?"

"Yes. Yes, it does."

"Then let's get going," Tony said. "Let's get going and have some fun."

They put their heads down and angled into the wind. Crossing the road wasn't half as easy as it looked.

Judge Osgood finished bundling Wisdom up in the buggy seat and then said, "I sure do thank you for what you're doing, Mr. Ramsey."

Matt just shrugged. "I just hope my luck holds."

"The road was pretty good?"

"Given all the snow, yes."

They were in the barn. The wind and snow ripped at the wood and threatened to tear the roof off. The place smelled sweetly of hay and kerosene.

Judge Osgood looked over at Wisdom again. He was so bundled up that he looked like a mummy that had been buried in red blankets. "I don't know how good his chances are."

"Neither do I," Matt said, "but we've got to find out."

"You really think Doc Ruark has enough strength to work on him?"

Matt nodded. "During the war I saw Doc work forty-eight hours in surgery with no sleep at all. And I saw him do it many times over. If anybody can get out of a deathbed and work on Wisdom here, it's Doc."

"Give him my best. He's a hell of a man."

Matt nodded and climbed up into the buggy. Judge

Osgood's servant had rubbed the horse down and given it some oats, preparing it for the second part of the perilous journey.

Judge Osgood went over and opened the barn doors. Or tried to. He finally had to have his servant help him. Pushing doors open against this kind of wind was nearly impossible.

And then once more Matt was out into the night. Every minute or so he'd check to see that Wisdom, propped up against him in the buggy seat, was doing all right. The buggy had a top that was already beginning to sag from the weight of the heavy, wet snow.

Matt had the sense that he was in this very narrow, endless tunnel. He also had the sense that he and the horse—and maybe Wisdom—were the only living beings on the entire planet. It was a nightmare.

Matt kept the horse running as straight as possible. The animal tended to lead them off into one of the huge drifts on the side of the road.

From time to time Matt saw cows that had drifted from surrounding ranches, only to get stuck in the snow and freeze to death. They looked like statues sticking up out of the snow.

Every few minutes Wisdom moaned, though whether in real pain or just delirium, Matt couldn't tell.

The progress down the road was slow beyond endurance. The horse kept her head down. Her metal shoes slipped easily on the slick surface. She nickered miserably, frightened by the noise of the wind and the sandlike grit of the snow on her head.

Again Matt was struck by how alone he felt. With no signs of any ranch house, no signs of any barbed wire even, the land probably looked much as it had when hairy mastodons pushed their way through at the beginning of the Ice Age.

And then the traces the horse was in felt loose suddenly, and Matt felt the animal skid off the road into a deep drift to the right.

Next to him, Wisdom moaned, as if even subconsciously he'd become aware of the bad turn their trip had taken.

The horse was in a panic, trying to extract herself from the snowdrift.

Matt jumped down from the buggy and went over to try and help the animal.

"Calm down, girl," he said. "Steady, girl."

The whole time he worked at using his hands as shovels, talking to the horse. He could see that his voice was calming the animal some.

The horse was buried to her knees.

Matt was squatted on his haunches, finally getting somewhere with the digging, when he heard the wail.

His first response was to run back to see how Wisdom was doing. In the murmuring wind, in the battering snow, the origin and exact nature of the wail were hard to define.

But Wisdom was quiet. Matt checked the young man's pulse. It was no better nor worse than it had been previously. The only thing that bothered Matt was the thin sheen of hot sweat that covered Wisdom's face. A body temperature this high in the middle of a freezing blizzard revealed just how poorly the kid was doing.

Matt stood in the center of the road, looking around.

In the dim moonlight, peering from behind clouds and the shifting curtain of snow, he saw how forlorn everything looked. It was impossible to imagine that the sky would ever be blue again or the ground green with grass and foliage.

And then the wail came again, and Matt knew that this was not a human sound.

At first he didn't see it—the animal he knew to be making the noise.

The snowfall was too heavy. But he sensed it drawing closer to him.

Matt took out his .44 and began scouting the area near the buggy. Every minute or so he had to wipe blinding snow from his face.

He knew what he was looking for.

The long snout.

The burning eyes.

The long, saliva-dripping teeth.

Timber wolf.

He walked several feet away from the buggy, his weapon drawn. He didn't give the animal sufficient credit for cunning, because that was exactly when the wolf struck.

The animal, knowing instinctively which of the two humans was the most vulnerable, leapt right for Wisdom.

The animal jumped up over the top of the buggy apron and landed on top of the unconscious lawman.

Matt knew he didn't dare shoot when the wolf was on top of Wisdom. Matt might kill Wisdom instead.

All Matt could do was rush up behind the animal and begin striking him across the skull with the barrel of his revolver.

At first the animal, so lost in his rage and frenzy, didn't even seem aware of Matt's presence.

But Matt made each successive blow harder, so at last the wolf started to show some effects from Matt's beating.

By now Wisdom was crying out. He sounded almost like an infant. The mauling had awakened him just enough to know that he was in a nightmare of pain. But even when he cried out, all one could hear was his delirium. He probably thought he'd died and gone to hell.

Matt lunged at the animal now, sinking his hands into the back of the wolf's neck.

Matt wasn't prepared for the strength he encountered. Big slabs of muscle shifted beneath the hairy coat. The stench of the wolf's saliva was fetid even in the coldness.

And then the animal turned away from the lawman and twisted around and flung himself at Matt.

Before he could defend himself in any way, the wolf had thrown Matt to the ground and was trying to sink his teeth into Matt's throat.

"Hello?"

"Mr. Carmody?"

"Yes."

"I have a message for you."

Jenna must have looked ghostly, standing there at the front door of Carmody's house.

The only illumination was from the kerosene lamp he bore. It shot a thin, golden shaft of light into the swirling blizzard surrounding the house.

Jenna had wrapped her cape and cowl so tightly around her that he couldn't see her face.

"What's the message?"

"An old friend of yours would like to see you tonight."

She could see that Carmody was plainly irritated. He had his winter coat on, ready to go out.

"What old friend?" he asked.

That's when Tony and Steve came around from the side of the house, their guns ready.

Carmody said, "What the hell is this?"

And then Jenna let her cowl drop back from her head.

At first he didn't recognize her. And this struck her as funny. You rape a very young girl—you take from her the most precious thing, next to life itself, that a young girl can possess—and then you see her again and don't even remember her.

But finally recognition came into his eyes and he said, "My God! Jenna!"

"Yes. It's me."

Tony put his Colt directly in Carmody's face. "Now you get in there before I blow that face of yours clean off. You understand me?"

Obviously, Carmody knew better than to argue.

He backed into his house once again and the three of them followed him, Tony first, keeping the gun right in Carmody's face.

The first thing Tony and Steve did was check out the house.

Tony whistled, obviously impressed. "You've got yourself a nice life here, mister."

"It's not what you think," Carmody said.

Tony guffawed. "Not what I think, huh? All this pretty furniture. All these fancy paintings. And a nice big fire-place like this. You should've seen some of the places I've lived in, mister, and then you'd know just how nice this place really is."

And with that, he took his Colt and shattered a vase into small pieces, debris flying through the air and smashing into the fireplace.

Jenna screamed.

"Take off your coat," Tony said to Carmody.

"Who the hell do you think you're talking to?" Carmody said.

Tony crossed the distance between them and struck Carmody hard enough on the jaw that the man's eyes rolled white.

Tony's skill at administering violence had always amazed Jenna. Tony wasn't especially big, nor did he look particularly strong, but once he decided to move in on somebody . . .

Carmody clutched at the couch to keep from falling to the floor.

"Take off your coat," Tony said. "Like I said, you ain't goin' nowhere."

Carmody obeyed.

"Steve," Tony said. "You start lookin' through the house. See what you can find. In the meantime here, I'm going to find out where Carmody keeps his wall safe."

Tony pointed the Colt directly at Carmody's chest. "And I'm also going to find out what the combination is."

Tony looked at Jenna. "You said he was a rich man, Jenna. Now I want to see him prove it."

And with that Carmody began to laugh.

It was a huge, unsettling laugh, and Tony wondered for a moment if the man hadn't lost his mind.

What the hell was so funny?

CHAPTER

★9★

The wolf had knocked Matt flat on his back in the snow.
Now the animal was only inches from his throat.

In the snowbound darkness of the blizzard, the wolf's
eyes seemed to glow with an almost supernatural hunger.

Matt pushed against the animal's jaw, the wolf's hot,
fetid saliva spraying across his face.

If Matt lost strength and let the wolf come closer . . .

The wolf growled low, anger tremoring through its
hunched, powerful body.

Matt had to regain his feet again so that he could draw
his weapon and fire at the animal.

And there was only one way to do this: take the chance
of rolling away from the wolf and then scramble quickly
to his feet.

Matt prepared himself as best he could. He clamped
down hard on the furry snout so that the wolf would
know Matt's strength and perhaps be somewhat leery
of the human.

And then Matt started pushing himself away through
the snow. He would have to move very quickly, and if
he failed in any way . . .

His jaws clamped shut, the wolf began again to growl.

Matt moved.

He started rolling away from the wolf, snow from the ground covering his face as he did so.

He heard the animal yelp and saw the gray beast lunge for him.

Feeling the wolf's body heat drawing near his own, Matt pitched himself to the right so that the arc of the descending animal missed him by half a foot.

Matt scrambled to his feet, drawing his weapon as he did so.

The wolf, getting himself reoriented after failing to grab onto Matt, crouched low once more, preparing himself to attack.

The eyes seemed to glow a pale red once more.

Even through the lashing snow, the silver saliva dripping from the long canine teeth was obvious.

Matt drew a bead on the animal and eased back the hammer.

But he didn't want to kill the wolf.

The animal was only responding to the stress of the storm. Under most circumstances, wolves left people alone.

But desperation had made this wolf crazy. If Matt let him go, the animal would probably attack the next human he saw.

The animal was crouching lower.

Growling deeper.

Before the animal jumped him and knocked him off his feet again, Matt had to make a choice.

And then the animal leapt.

Matt shot him in the side, just above his right rear haunch.

The wolf's sound of pain overwhelmed even the bitter, blowing wind.

Matt had no trouble stepping aside and letting the

wolf's arc carry him over next to a poplar tree, where he tumbled into the snow.

There the animal thrashed around on the ground, furious but too stunned to get himself ready for another attack.

Matt went over and stood above the animal.

He wanted to bend down and pet the wolf and reassure him that human and wolf could be friends. But the animal still had great rage in him, and he could certainly kill Matt if he got the proper chance.

But Matt was glad he'd decided to simply wound and waylay the animal. The wolf was too honorable a beast to kill frivolously.

Nodding a farewell to the wolf, Matt trudged through the snow back to the buggy.

He lifted the mummylike blankets that covered young Wisdom and checked him over. His pulse remained faint but steady, and warm sweat still bathed his face.

Matt knew that time was getting more precious by the second.

Without proper medical help, Wisdom didn't have long to live. And maybe even with the proper medical help, the young man wouldn't make it anyway. The human body didn't easily sustain three serious gunshot wounds.

Matt then returned to the frightened horse, who was trying uselessly to free herself from the snowbank. She tossed her body back and forth so violently, Matt was afraid she would snap one of her legs.

Matt went up to the animal and began stroking her gently on the crest, talking directly into her ear so that she could hear the reassuring rhythms of Matt's speech.

Then Matt knelt down and began digging the animal's forelegs out of the snow again.

In all, it took twenty minutes of freezing, blinding

work. Several times Matt had to stop and get up and begin stroking the horse and talking to her again. The blizzard had made the animal crazy with fear.

Finally Matt was able to get the traces tightened on the horse again, and he set the animal and buggy aright on the trail.

He climbed up next to Wisdom on the buggy seat and then urged the horse onward.

There was a long, nervous moment when the animal did nothing at all but merely stood with her head lowered against the icy blast of snow and wind.

But at last the horse picked up the shank of one leg and then the shank of the other and slowly, very slowly, began making its way down the road.

Wisdom, seeming to understand what was going on in some subconscious way, made a soft gurgling sound in his throat.

Matt looked over at Wisdom and smiled.

They had a long way to go before they reached Doc Ruark's place.

Matt just hoped Wisdom could last that long.

Since both of Dowd's deputies were busy fighting the blizzard, Dowd himself had to make a sweep of the town. He was not used to this sort of public-minded role. To him, being sheriff meant wielding power and enjoying the privileges of that power.

He wasn't enjoying himself.

An hour before, he'd had to help shovel free a wagon with a mother and six children. Half an hour before, he'd had to go into a barn and put out a small fire that had started in the loft.

Now—his deputies working with a family whose roof had collapsed under the heavy snow—Dowd walked around town carrying a lantern, seeing if there were anybody outside and in distress.

His tour of the mountain was good for one thing, anyway. It helped get his mind off the showdown that was coming. Dowd was a realist. He knew that he'd long enjoyed the fruits of being sheriff of Templar without paying any penalty for his excesses.

Well, now that penalty was coming due. Wisdom had to be killed, otherwise he would lead a revolt against Dowd, and the sheriff and Carmody would end up one cold gray morning standing on a scaffold with ropes around their necks.

He hoped that Carmody was on his way to taking care of that now. He shouldn't have any trouble intercepting Matt Ramsey and Wisdom on their return trip to town and killing them.

Dowd went on his way, a fat, grotesque silhouette in the eerie glow of the lantern he carried as made his way through the lashing snowstorm.

And then he came to Carmody's house and he couldn't believe what he saw.

There, silhouetted behind a gauzy curtain, was Carmody.

Why the hell hadn't he ridden out to kill Ramsey and Wisdom?

What the hell was he doing still snug and comfortable in his house?

Angered, Dowd started walking across the street, ready to pound on Carmody's door and demand an explanation.

But that was when the screaming started.

It came from somewhere behind Dowd, somewhere in the snow-lost darkness that enveloped this entire mountain community.

Who was screaming? And why?

Much as he hated to, Dowd had to play at being

sheriff. Forget seeing Carmody and go see what the hell was going on.

Gripping the kerosene lantern, Dowd turned his bulk around in the gloom and set off in the direction of the screams that were still as loud as the furious wind itself.

The west was filled with urchins like these, Carmody thought, looking at Jenna and Tony and Steve.

Jenna and Steve sat almost politely on the couch while Tony leaned against the fireplace. He kept his gun trained steadily on Carmody.

"We want valuables we can carry in a gunny sack," Tony said. "And if you don't come through for us, you're going to be dead in short order."

Carmody continued pouring himself a snifter of brandy. He enjoyed the fact that his coolness upset Tony, who had obviously expected Carmody to be frightened.

Carmody looked over at Jenna and Steve. They sat almost primly, hands in their laps, looking from Tony to Carmody. They looked embarrassed and they looked afraid. Tony was the outlaw here, not these two. They were just followers.

Carmody found great amusement in all this.

Here Jenna, a girl he'd raped before she was even ten year old, had waited all these years to pay him back. She would show up on his doorstep with two vermin who would hold him up for his money.

And that would be her vengeance.

At Carmody's expense, she would become wealthy. At least for a time. Until some outlaw she'd fallen under the spell of stole it all from her. Carmody saw how she stared at Tony: part love and part terror. And at the moment, she appeared to be having serious second thoughts about love.

"Where's your safe?" Tony asked.

Carmody glanced at him, then set the brandy decanter down. "You expect me to put up some kind of fight, don't you?" Amusement was strong in his voice. Amusement was too subtle for Tony. Anger he would have understood easily enough. But amusement? Confusion played on Tony's face. "Well, I'm not going to. I'm going to walk straight over to the wall safe and show you just where it's at."

Steve and Jenna exchanged glances.

Tony said, "Another couple of minutes, you won't be laughing at all, asshole."

Carmody nodded toward Jenna. "Such nice friends you have, Jenna. They make me seem almost decent by comparison, don't they?"

He saw Jenna flush. She'd probably been thinking something similar herself.

Carmody set his brandy snifter down and walked across the room to a large portrait of himself.

"You'll have to excuse the vanity," he said. Then he smiled at Jenna. "I suppose you remember this from . . . our night together, eh? Actually, I find it quite flattering."

Tony looked just as confused as ever. In his world, there were two kinds of men: gentlemen and outlaws. The former tended to be nellies and the latter hard cases. He'd never met a man before with the manners of a gentleman and the scruples of an outlaw. Carmody had always prided himself on the way he combined these traits. People didn't expect it, and surprise was always the most formidable weapon of all.

Carmody swung the portrait back on unseen hinges, revealing a large, gray, circular wall safe.

"Hey," Steve said. "There it is!"

He sounded as excited as a child. He got up from the

couch and began moving sluggishly toward the wall safe, as if he'd just been hypnotized.

Tony shoved him. "I'm taking care of this. You go back there and sit down."

Steve cursed Tony and glowered at him, but he went back and sat down next to Jenna.

"What's in there?" Tony wanted to know.

"You'll be surprised."

Carmody sounded as amused and droll as ever.

"I don't like surprises, mister."

"Well, you're about to get one. And a big one."

Carmody thought again of all the years that poor, pale Jenna had planned this night of vengeance. To take from Carmody the things Carmody found most precious: his earthly possessions. But then to find out that Carmody was broke!

"You open that goddamn thing and you open it right now. You hear me?"

"I hear you. I'm just trying to warn you."

"You keep your warning to yourself." Tony waved his gun at Carmody for emphasis.

Carmody put his hand up to the dial.

And then he paused. "I should tell you now."

"Tell me what?"

"That I have no money."

Tony laughed bitterly. His eyes swept the fancy room. "You don't have no money? You really expect me to believe that?"

"Oh, I'm not surprised you're taken in by all the furnishings. This is a beautiful house; there's no denying that. But you asked for things you could take away in a gunny sack, and I'm afraid there isn't much of that."

Carmody turned to face Jenna, now that he had completed his little speech.

He wanted to see her face when he told her the sad

truth about his financial affairs.

Carmody said, "I'm bankrupt."

And he instantly saw that she knew he was telling the truth.

Tony went into a kind of spasm. "What the hell're you talkin' about, bankrupt? Jenna says you're one of the richest men in these mountains."

"Past tense." Carmody shook his head, and here his air of worldly amusement lessened. Not even he could smile when he recalled how ineptly he'd run his financial affairs. "One bad investment at a time. I wouldn't listen to anybody. No, I had to do it my way. And then suddenly I woke up one day and found that I couldn't even get credit anymore." He smiled sadly at Jenna, as if playing to an audience. "You can imagine what it's been like for me. My pride especially. When you've been the richest man in the mountains, people don't forgive you when you lose your money. As much as they resented you for your money, they actually wanted you to keep it because it gave them something to dream of. But now that you don't have any money . . . well, they hate you even more than they did before."

Tony struck Carmody then.

He pulled back his Colt and then brought the barrel down on Carmody's jawline. The movement was swift, expert.

Carmody wobbled against the wall, almost pitching over. The force of the blow had been considerable.

Jenna said, "You didn't need to do that."

"You must forget who this bugger is, Jenna," Tony said. "This is the man who raped you when you was a little girl."

"I know. But still—"

"If I was you I'd want him to die," Tony said. Then he looked at Carmody straightening himself up. "He just might die anyway if he don't come up with some greenbacks real soon."

Now Steve got up from the couch. "Jenna's right, Tony. No cause to hurt him." Steve still had nightmares about a hanging Tony had taken him to. Steve still feared that he himself would end up on a gallows some day.

"You remember what I said a while ago?" Tony asked.

"Huh?" Steve said.

"You go back there on that goddamn couch and keep your mouth shut. You hear me?"

Steve looked as if he'd been slapped.

He trudged back to the couch and sat down.

Jenna was still on her feet. She said, "You're not lying, are you?"

"No," Carmody said, touching his sore jaw.

"You're really broke?"

Carmody nodded.

"I should be very happy."

"Yes, you should," Carmody said. "You've had your vengeance. Unless my luck changes considerably, I'll end up a destitute old man."

"But you still won't give a damn what you did to me, will you?" Jenna said.

She stared directly into his eyes.

She saw nothing there. They were striking, even handsome blue eyes. But there was no feeling in them. She imagined his heart was just as empty.

She said to Tony, "Why don't we go?"

"Go? Are you crazy? We came here for loot, and by God we're not leaving till we have some."

"He's broke, Tony. You heard him."

"You believe him? He's lying."

"I don't think so, Tony."

And then he slapped her. The blow was vicious, and it knocked her back three feet.

"You better fuckin' pray he's got money, bitch, because if he don't, I'm gonna kill you both. And you'd better believe I mean what I'm sayin' too, bitch."

And she did, of course.

For the first time, she saw Tony for what he was: a true criminal, a killer, just as hard and crazed and immoral as Carmody.

"You get over there and stand next to him, Jenna," Tony said. "He's gonna open the safe now, and there had better by God be somethin' in there. You understand me?"

CHAPTER

★10★

When Dowd finally reached the source of the screaming, he found that a kitchen fire had started in the house closest to Carmody's.

A woman stood in the living room and screamed as her husband started carrying shovelsful of snow in from outdoors and throwing them on the fire.

It was going to be a while before the volunteer fire department got organized.

Sheriff Dowd had no choice but to be a good citizen. He grabbed an extra shovel and started helping the man put out the blaze that had started when some cooking grease had gone up in flames.

It wasn't a serious fire, but it required some time and patience.

He tried not to think about why Carmody was still in his house, why he hadn't gone out to kill Wisdom and Ramsey.

"I want to thank you for helpin' us this way," the grateful home owner said. He couldn't keep the surprise from his voice. Sheriff Dowd wasn't exactly known as a big help to the community.

"That's all right," Dowd said, enjoying his moment of esteem. "I'm just doin' my duty."

But the woman of the house, more cynical than her husband, looked at Dowd and smirked. He was treacherous, true, but he was also foolish in his way.

Winona stood in the doorway of her father's room, holding a small kerosene lamp that threw golden reflections across the white walls.

She wondered if she'd done the right thing, volunteering her father as Wisdom's doctor.

Was she being selfish?

Maybe she was so concerned about Wisdom that she wasn't paying proper attention to her father.

Maybe instead of helping him, she was only hastening his death. Maybe the shock of getting out of bed and performing surgery would only kill him faster.

Setting the lamp down on the edge of the bureau, she walked over to her father's bed and took a seat next to him.

She put a small hand on his hip and smiled at the way he looked almost young just now, sleeping so soundly.

She had so many good memories of this man. When he died, he would take a very big part of her world with him.

So now she had to wonder again. Had she done the right thing by telling Matt that she'd help get her father out of bed, so that he could take Wisdom's bullets out?

As if in answer, wind and snow slammed into the small house like a fist.

She thought of Wisdom out there in the raging night.

And she knew that she had indeed done the right thing.

Her father was a man of medicine, a healer, and that had been his pride all his life.

He would take great pleasure in getting up from his deathbed and trying to save a life.

Hurry, she thought. *Hurry.*

She didn't know how much longer Wisdom would last with his wounds.

Nor did she know how much longer her father would last as he slipped in and out of consciousness.

Hurry.

Carmody reached over and deftly opened the wall safe. Three quick turns, two right, one left.

And it was open.

"Now you get back from there," Tony said.

Carmody's smile remained ironic. "You still don't believe me yet?"

"I said get out of the way."

"It's empty, my friend. Just like my bank account. Just like my pockets. Empty."

He looked at Jenna and smiled, as if she alone had the intelligence and grace to understand what he was saying.

Tony shoved Carmody aside and walked up to the safe.

And stuck his hand into the round dark hole.

And wiggled his fingers around.

And said, "You sonofabitch."

"Why are you cursing me?" Carmody said mildly. "I told you just what you'd find: nothing."

"Where the hell are your greenbacks?"

"Scattered all over the United States in investments that didn't work."

"You're lyin'," Tony said, moving toward the bigger man.

"I only wish I were," Carmody said. "If I had a trunkful of greenbacks somewhere I'd be glad to give you half. Glad to. Because that would mean that the other half were mine."

Tony shot him then, without warning and, judging by Tony's hard expression, any regret either.

Jenna screamed.

Tony looked at her. "What the hell's wrong with you?"

"There was no need to shoot him like that."

Tony shook his head. "I thought this was the man you hated so much."

"He is. But still . . ."

She couldn't explain her confused feelings. True, she did hate Carmody. And she did want to see him brought to justice. But that didn't mean that she wanted to see Tony beat him half to death.

Tony took a pleasure in violence that was ugly to see.

Just now, watching Tony shoot Carmody, she realized she'd made a bad mistake.

She did not love Tony after all. Now, in fact, she hated him. And feared him.

And she should never have brought him to this town or this house.

Even given what Carmody had done to her, he did not deserve the punishment Tony was meting out to him. She could see that Carmody was still alive, holding his side where he'd been shot.

Steve spoke up. "She's right, Tony. He must be tellin' the truth. If he had any money he'd tell us."

What Jenna saw in Tony's eyes just then horrified her.

She'd long sensed Tony's contempt for Steve. He used Steve as his servant but little else.

Now she saw that Tony's contempt for the slow-witted Steve was much deeper than she'd imagined.

"Is that right, bright boy? Is that how you read this situation?"

Steve saw how angry Tony was. He tried apologizing. "All I meant to say was—"

"Stand up."

"What?"

"Get your ass up off that couch."

"But Tony, I—"

"You goddamn do what I say!" Tony shouted.

And Steve instantly obeyed him.

And Tony shot him.

One bullet, directly in the heart, was all it took.

Steve went over backward, arms flailing for balance, his face kidlike and astonished that somebody he'd looked up to so much could possibly have done this.

This time Jenna didn't scream.

She just stood there, silently crying.

And when Steve fell sprawling over the couch, she hurried to him, to see if there were any way she could make his last moments more peaceful.

Steve had already fouled his pants. That and the stench of warm blood mixed together almost overwhelmed Jenna as she lay the cool palm of her hand on Steve's forehead.

He couldn't talk.

He was in the last seconds of his existence, standing on the very precipice of dark and eternal extinction.

He looked like a frightened animal, his blue eyes huge and pleading and terrified.

And then he died.

Just like that.

Jenna had never seen anybody die before, and she was almost fascinated by the process.

One moment you were alive and talking and—

"Don't start cryin'," Tony said, coming over by her now. "And get up from there and leave him alone."

Jenna rose with all the dignity she could muster and looked straight at Tony. "You don't even know, do you?"

"Know what?"

"That you're insane."

He laughed. "Is that the word for it?"

"He cared for you, and you didn't even know it."

"He was stupid."

Very quietly, Jenna said, "He was your friend, Tony."

He waved the gun toward the spiral staircase. "You go upstairs and see what you can find."

She looked over at Carmody, slumped unconscious against the wall by the open safe. "He's telling the truth. He's broke."

Tony took a threatening step toward her. "You bitch! You talked me into comin' to this town because you said he had all this money!"

"I didn't know that he'd blown it all on bad investments."

Tony waved his gun again. "You get upstairs, bitch, and start lookin' for stuff we can take."

Tony nodded toward Steve's corpse. "Otherwise in a few minutes, you're gonna look just like him."

By the time Matt reached Doc Ruark's place, Wisdom had started moaning. Matt wasn't sure why.

He pulled the buggy up in front of the house and then jumped down to take Wisdom inside.

The young lawman seemed even heavier now than he had before.

Carrying Wisdom in his arms, Matt went up to the Ruark front door and knocked by kicking the point of one Texas boot against the door.

Winona came to the door, the gusting wind nearly knocking her over.

She held the door wide for Matt. He brought Wisdom inside and carried him over to the couch, which Winona had fixed up with sheets and blankets as a bed.

He was happy to lay Wisdom down.

Winona looked anxiously at Matt and asked, "Is he . . ."

"Still alive as far as I can tell."

"Did he say anything?"

"Nothing coherent."

Her voice conveyed her anxiety. "I got worried when you were gone. It looks bad out there."

"You'd have to be out in that snow to appreciate it."

She looked down at Wisdom. "You think he's handsome, Matt?"

"A regular kewpie doll."

Winona smiled. "I can't help it, Matt. I've had this terrible crush on him most of my life."

She came to his outstretched arms and said, "Do you want to go in and talk to my father?"

"Sure."

"He doesn't know yet—about Wisdom, I mean."

"I'll tell him."

"You think he's strong enough?"

"I think he'd be very mad if he knew we let him sleep while a young man was dying out here."

"That's what I think too," she said.

Matt gave her a squeeze and then went into the bedroom.

He didn't turn up the kerosene lamp. He just stood in the darkness, listening to the soft, wet snoring of his old friend.

His old dying friend.

Matt went over to the bureau and picked up the lamp and brought it over to the bedside.

Clifton was on his back. His eyes were closed. His long, slender hands lay one over the other on his stomach. It was easy enough to imagine him in a coffin.

"Clifton."

Nothing.

"Clifton."

Still nothing.

"Clifton. It's me, Matt."

And then the first stirring.

The eyelids starting to flicker.

The mouth parting.

"Clifton. There's a young man I brought back here. He needs a doctor, Clifton."

And then the eyes came full open.

At first Clifton looked disoriented, as if he'd already died and was just now coming awake in the other realm.

He looked up. "Matt?"

"Right here."

Clifton's eyes went to the window. "I've never heard it blow like that before."

"It's pretty bad."

"Winona awake?"

Obviously Clifton didn't remember what Matt had told him about the wounded man. "She's in the living room with Wisdom."

"Wisdom came calling on a night like this?"

"Wisdom's been shot, Clifton."

"What?"

"And shot pretty bad, too. He needs a doctor."

And all of a sudden, recognition came into Clifton's eyes. "A doctor?"

"That's right."

"I'm the only doctor in this town."

"That's why I woke you up."

"The bullets are still in him?"

"Yep. You think you've got the strength to get them out?"

"I'd sure like to try."

"I'm sure your daughter would appreciate it."

Clifton stared at him for a long moment. "You'll have to help me, Matt."

"I know."

"I haven't even been able to stand up for the past four days."

Matt nodded.

Clifton sighed. "I just don't want to hurt him any worse than he's hurt already."

"I wouldn't worry about that. He's taken three shots."

"Who did it?"

"Dowd or Carmody or both of them."

Matt told him about the warrant for Carmody's arrest.

"My God," Clifton said.

"What?"

"It's finally happening. Carmody and Dowd are losing their power."

Knowing this seemed to give Clifton a sudden jolt of strength.

He carefully moved one pale, shaky leg out from under the covers.

"I'm just wearing drawers is all, Matt."

Matt grinned. "I'm shocked."

"My pants're over there. Can you get them for me?"

Matt felt bad as hell for the other man. Now that he was up on his legs, Clifton looked more emaciated and powerless than ever.

Matt went over and got Clifton his pants, then helped get them on. Clifton had to draw his belt to the last notch in order for his pants to stay up.

"She got him on the couch?"

"Yep," Matt said.

"She acted as my nurse a lot of times. She'll know about getting the bandages and the hot water."

Matt started helping him out of the room. "She tells me she's got this big crush on him," he said.

Clifton snorted. "That doesn't come as news to me. She's had this crush on him ever since he was three."

"That's a long time."

Clifton looked at Matt and smiled. "Hopefully they'll be married even longer than that."

Then they went out into the living room to see what they could do for the young lawman.

CHAPTER
11

Jenna felt trapped in a nightmare. She wished she had never come back to this town, never met Tony, never decided to seek vengeance for her rape.

She even wished she had not tried to become an actress.

How comforting it would be on night such as this, one filled with bloodshed and blizzards, to sit in front of the hearth with your own family and enjoy hot cocoa while the elements slammed furiously at the roof and windows.

Tony had sent her upstairs looking for valuables in Carmody's rooms. She had been through three rooms now and had found nothing. Carmody hadn't been kidding. He had stripped his house bare to sell things off for cash. There was nothing left except the necessities.

As she moved through the rooms, searching in closets and drawers, the house had the feel of a place up for rent.

She left the master bedroom empty-handed and went down the hall to the den.

Even many of the books were gone. Half the shelves stood empty.

In the dust on a cupboard she could see where vases had once sat, but now they were gone.

It was then that she glanced out the window and got the idea.

With Steve dead—and she would never forget the completely indifferent way in which Tony had shot his friend—she had nobody to turn to.

She had to get out of this house.

There was no way she was going to escape Tony when Tony was around.

She walked over to the window.

But what if she could push the window up and crawl out onto the roof and jump two floors to safety?

Certainly she could escape this way.

And by the time she was gone, it would be too late for Tony to do anything.

She leaned over and tried to push up the window.

It didn't budge.

Moisture and freezing temperatures had stuck it to its frame.

She went over to the desk and searched through the drawers till she found a paper opener.

She brought the daggerlike instrument back to the window and began running the sharp edge up and down the window frame.

At one point Tony came to the bottom of the stairs and shouted, "How's it going up there?"

"I'm almost finished," she shouted back.

And then she started working even harder at loosening the window.

She could hear the ice beginning to shear away. Now when she brought all her force to the window and tried to push it up, she could also feel it begin to give a little.

A few more passes with the letter opener and she'd—

And then she heard the footsteps.

Tony. Coming up the steps. "What the hell're you doing up here?"

His voice was loud, echoing off the narrow hallway.

She dropped the letter opener into the pocket of her dress and hurried out of the room.

Tony stood in the shadows of the hallway, holding a kerosene lamp. "What're you doing, anyway?" His voice was thick with accusation.

"Just what you told me to: I'm looking for valuables."

Tony stared at her. "You sure?"

"Of course. What else would I be doing?"

"You been up here a long time."

"Just a few more minutes is all I need."

Her eyed her carefully. "You know what I done to Steve."

She shuddered. "Yes."

"Well I'll do the same thing to you if you try anything funny."

"I know."

He looked around at the rooms off the hallway. "You find anything yet?"

"Not yet."

"You picked some good goddamned place to rob."

"I didn't know he was broke."

Tony scowled. "He'll be more than broke when I get done with him. I'll promise you that."

He held the kerosene lamp up so that shadows leapt playfully along the hallway. "You be quick about it. I'll be downstairs. I've got him tied up to a chair but I still don't trust him."

"All right."

He looked at her for a long time again, almost as if he could read her mind and see what she was really thinking.

And then he lowered the lamp and turned around and walked down the stairs again.

She immediately went back to the den.

She took out the knife and started working it along the edge of the window frame.

Her heart pounded. Her entire body was covered with cold sweat.

She knew that if Tony ever caught her doing this . . .

She tried not to think about that. She wanted to concentrate only on the job at hand.

She angled the knife through the ice that had collected along the frame, then every minute or so she'd try pushing up the window once again.

Each time it pushed up a little easier.

One of these times . . .

There!

This time when she pushed she could feel it shift free from its moorings and begin to slide upward.

It would be so easy to climb out through the window and get on the roof and . . .

She pushed the window all the way up.

The snow and wind roaring through the open window pushed her back a few feet.

In just a few seconds, her face and hands were numb from the raw elements.

She raised one leg, smiling at herself for being so unladylike.

There was just no graceful or proper way to climb through the window and out on the roof.

So she forgot all about the fact that she'd spent her life trying very hard to be a lady.

She raised one foot and got it on the sill and started to pull herself through.

And that was when Tony came out of the blackness behind her.

"You bitch!" he cried.

He grabbed her face from behind and hurled her painfully backward. She slammed into a wall and then slowly sank to the floor. Her head spun. She felt nauseous. But mostly she felt terrified. After what Tony had done to Steve, she knew that Tony was perfectly capable of doing anything.

He'd have no hesitation about killing a woman.

As if to confirm her thoughts, Tony came across the floor, his Colt dangling from his right hand. He raised a booted foot and kicked her hard in the ribs.

She cried out, grabbing her midsection and doubling over.

The pain was incredible, arcing upward across her ribs and even shooting up and down her right arm.

And then Tony kicked her again, this time a clear hard shot in the side of the head.

"You bitch!" he said again.

Her head buzzed and the sudden blackness in front of her eyes led to panic. What if Tony had blinded her permanently?

Whorls of stars and other patterns whirled in front of her eyes. She could hear everything in the room: the wind and snow still roaring, the floorboards creaking as Tony moved around. But she could see nothing, nothing.

"You think I didn't know you was up to something?" Tony said. "You're dumber than I thought."

But she wasn't paying any attention.

Her only reality was the pounding pain in her skull from where he'd kicked her and the utter darkness before her eyes.

"I should kill you right now," he said.

And she almost wanted to cry out: *Then do it! Do it now and get it over with!*

But she didn't, of course. Terrified as she was, she didn't want to die.

She heard him make some sudden move and then he was right next to her, kneeling by her.

He lashed her hands behind her with rope. He pulled the bonds so tight her circulation was immediately halved.

"You won't be goin' nowhere this time, believe me."

He stood up.

She still couldn't see anything.

She started crying.

This had all gone so wrong. There was no money to pay for the vengeance she'd wanted. And Steve was dead.

And now she was tied up.

And blind. Blind!

"You won't be goin' nowhere, bitch," Tony said, and then he left her in the room alone with the howling wind and snow and the utter darkness before her eyes.

After he'd been fighting the fire for an hour, Dowd was joined by a few other neighbors. What could have been a disaster was contained and became little more than a minor kitchen fire.

Several of the neighbors who'd helped quell the flames smiled at each other when they saw Dowd puffing himself up and taking most of the credit.

"I just read an article a couple weeks ago about how to put out fires like these," he said. "Good thing I subscribe to that magazine or we'd never have gotten it out."

The citizens smiled some more to themselves.

Dowd's contribution had largely consisted of throwing some water on the flames every ten minutes or so while the others did the more serious—and ultimately more important—work of putting sand on the fire and keeping the flames contained to a single room in the house.

Dowd had capped off the evening predictably. He asked the man who owned the house if he happened to have any bourbon on hand. Dowd's tone of voice implied that he well deserved a drink. The way Dowd eyed the man's wife even hinted that maybe twenty minutes in the sack with this lady might not be totally out of line either.

Dowd was drinking his third shot of whiskey and just remembering that he'd better get over and see what was going on at Carmody's when a new neighbor showed up with news.

"You hear about Wisdom?"

"No, what about him?" a man said.

"Shot."

"Shot! Holy gosh! When?"

"Couple hours ago," the new neighbor said.

"Know who did it?"

"Nope."

Though the house was filled with smoke and the smell of burned wood, everybody stood around as if there were a party in progress. And, in a way, there was.

Now, though, everybody looked at Dowd.

"Afraid I don't know nothin' about it," Dowd said. "Maybe I'd better go check this out. Is he—dead?"

"Nope. He's over at Doc Ruark's."

Doc Ruark's! Dowd thought. What the hell was Carmody doing? He was supposed to have killed both Wisdom and Ramsey by now.

"I'll go look into things," Dowd said.

And people smiled at each other again, at this chest-puffing display of competence and concern Dowd some-times like to put on.

Before he left, he took the time to down one more drink of whiskey. A big one.

At the door, he looked at the husband and wife who lived here and said, "I'm glad I saw the flames and came over. God only knows what would have happened if I hadn't."

The people in the house had the courtesy to hold their laughter until Dowd had closed the door behind him.

Dowd couldn't remember ever seeing snow like this. It lashed at him, tearing into his skin, and numbing it too.

The wind threatened to bowl him off his feet, leave him flailing on his back in the white fury of the night.

Dowd trudged through knee-deep snow toward Carmody's house.

Dowd still wondered what the hell was going on. Why hadn't Wisdom and Ramsey been killed?

The last time he'd looked, Carmody had been silhouetted in one of the front windows.

Now the curtains were drawn heavily across the windows. Only a faint light could be seen behind them.

Dowd stood in the whipping snow and had a terrible premonition that something inside was wrong.

Seriously wrong.

His hand dropped to the aged Peacemaker riding in his holster.

Hell, he was sheriff of this burg. What did he have to be afraid of?

Just as another swooping volley of wind came at him, Dowd set his foot on what was normally the boardwalk and set off for Carmody's house.

Given Carmody's drinking habits, maybe all that had happened was that he'd started drinking and then started thinking better of killing two men.

Over the years Carmody and Dowd had been involved in a lot of graft, but they'd never killed anybody. Not anybody white, anyway. Dowd sometimes took great pleasure in killing Chinee, but that wasn't like killing real people at all.

He went up to Carmody's house, raised the brass knocker, and slammed it against its metal base.

Even through the howling noise of the snow and wind, one could hear the metallic thudding of the knocker.

No way could Carmody fail to respond.

Inside, having finished tying up Jenna, Tony was coming downstairs when he heard the knock.

Sonofabitch, he thought. Who'd be out and about on a night like this?

Tony's only thoughts now were to cover his tracks, to kill both Jenna and Carmody and get out of town before the storm stopped.

A blizzard might scare some people, but for Tony it offered the perfect cover for his escape.

The brass knocker sounded again.

Who the hell could it be?

There was only one way to find out, of course.

Tony came downstairs. The first place he checked was the dining room. Carmody was tied up very neatly, bound and gagged, in the east corner.

Carmody's blue eyes had an almost pathetic pleading in them. Carmody knew he was about to be murdered.

Tony, satisfied that Carmody wouldn't be any problem, went over to the door and listened.

"Carmody!" a voice came. "Carmody! Open up! It's me! Dowd!"

And then Tony smiled.

Maybe his luck was turning around after all. True, he wasn't going to get much in the way of cash from this job, but he'd finally ridded himself of that clinging pest Steve. And now he knew he was going to get his chance to pay back that fat-ass sheriff who'd humiliated him that afternoon.

Tony pushed his face tight against the door. Between the wind and muffling his voice, there was no way Dowd could tell who was speaking.

"I'll open the door and then you run in!" he called.

"Just hurry up! I'm freezin' my balls off out here."

"Hold on," Tony said, muffling his voice again.

He stood behind the door, put his hand on the knob, and then pulled it open.

Riding a crest of wind and snow, Dowd was blown inside.

The squat lawman looked around, confused.

Obviously he was wondering where the hell his friend Carmody was.

He couldn't see behind the door.

And then Tony slammed it.

And then he stood there with his Colt pointed right at Dowd's fat stomach.

"Hello, Sheriff." Tony grinned.

And then he brought the handle of his gun viciously down on Dowd's mouth, shattering several teeth and giving the man a choking throatful of his own thick blood.

"We're gonna have some fun, you and me," Tony said.

He pushed the sheriff into the living room.

CHAPTER

⋆12⋆

He had just leaned over the couch, a scalpel trembling in his hand, when he pitched forward and fell across Wisdom's body.

Winona screamed.

Matt got his hands on Clifton's frail body and raised him up off the wounded man.

Matt gathered Clifton up and carried him into the bedroom, laying him out comfortably on top of the mussed bedclothes.

Winona came right behind, a kerosene lantern in her hand.

She set it down on the night table and asked Matt to move aside and then she began checking her father over to see if he was all right.

At first Matt felt that Clifton might have died. Winona wasn't able to get any response from him whatsoever.

At one point she picked up his limp arm and checked his pulse. Though she said nothing, a small frown creased her mouth.

Winona and Matt stood side by side over Clifton's bed, saying nothing, just listening to the wind and snow batter the house.

They had taken him out there to save Wisdom's life, but maybe they had been selfish. Clifton clearly wasn't up to the job. He had been on his feet less than five minutes and he'd collapsed from utter and complete exhaustion.

Now Winona looked at Matt. "Neither one of them will live through the night," she said quietly.

Matt reached out and took the small woman into his arms. He gave her a hug. "People have a way of surprising you."

And just then, Clifton did surprise them.

First his eyes came open. Then he spoke.

"I'm sorry I passed out," he said shakily.

"It's all right, Father. You did your best. Now just lie there and be comfortable."

"I want to try again."

"No!" Winona said. Her voice was like a gunshot. "You're not well enough to try again."

Clifton looked up at her with his haunted, dying eyes. "Honey, you're forgetting something."

"What?"

"I'm a doctor."

"Oh, Father, you really shouldn't get up out of bed."

Clifton looked up at Matt and smiled. "You want to tell her how stubborn I was during the war?"

Matt laughed. "He isn't kidding you, Winona. He used to work till he'd fall asleep on his feet."

"You just don't have the strength," Winona said.

Clifton shook his head. "Get me some whiskey."

"What?"

"Please, honey, just do what I say."

"How's whiskey going to help?"

"If I can keep a few belts down, that'll give me enough energy to get through the worst of it. From what I saw out there, the bullets won't be too difficult to take out once I get going. The angles are reasonably accessible, anyway."

Winona glanced at Matt.

Matt nodded.

Winona went and got the whiskey.

"I don't want both of her men to die," Clifton said when they were alone. "I'd always kind of counted on Wisdom being here when I was gone, and dammit, I want to make sure that actually happens."

"You're a good man, Clifton."

Clifton smiled. "You always have to go and get sentimental, don't you, Matthew?"

Winona came back with a quart of good bourbon and a glass.

Matt helped prop Clifton up in bed. Matt poured him two fingersful of liquor.

Clifton took the glass and frowned. "You afraid I'm going to get drunk and make a fool of myself? How about pouring me a little more?"

Matt laughed. "See, Winona, just what I told you. He's using all this as an excuse to get drunk."

Winona shook her head. "I can't imagine what you two were like in the war together."

Matt poured Clifton more whiskey. "You wouldn't want to know, believe me."

Clifton drank half the whiskey in the glass and then leaned back against the headboard.

"This stuff sure has a kick," he said. "My head's spinning and my chest feels like it's on fire."

Matt also noticed that Clifton's voice had become richer and fuller, more like it was normally.

"I'd better go check on Wisdom," Winona said.

After she'd gone, Clifton said, "I want to give it my best try, Matt."

"You mean with Wisdom?"

Clifton nodded.

"I'll help you all I can."

"All I'm saying is, don't pamper me. Let me work till I drop." Clifton put out a hand. "Now help this old bastard to his feet so he can get to work."

"You sure?"

"I'm sure."

Matt had to admit that Clifton felt surer on his feet this time than he had before.

Matt helped him take one step, two, three.

Winona came back into the bedroom. "His pulse is getting worse."

"Then we'd better work fast," Clifton said.

Matt stayed on one side, Winona went over to the other, and together they helped him into the living room.

Before they'd had to hand Clifton his instruments.

This time he did most of his prep work by himself. Winona and Matt got Wisdom's bloody shirt off him and then covered him with a white sheet to help keep him from chilling. His flesh was very hot to the touch.

Clifton picked up his scalpel.

"How are you feeling, Father?"

Clifton smiled. "It's amazing what a little whiskey can do for a man. I should have been prescribing that to my patients all these years." He looked down at Wisdom stretched out in front of him. "Well, after he wakes up, let's see how he feels about being operated on by a drunken surgeon."

And with that, Clifton began.

Matt thought of trying to help, but he soon saw there was nothing he could do except make sure that plenty of boiling water was kept on hand.

A couple of times Clifton looked as if he were going to pass out again.

Matt rushed to him and held him up till he felt strong again.

Wisdom seemed about to come awake a few times. He moaned and coughed and once he cried out, his voice lost and childlike in the silence.

Clifton worked with amazing diligence.

All Matt could think of was the long hours Clifton had put in during the war. The floor of the surgery tent had run with blood and flies had formed a moving black ring around the canvas structure. Day became night and night became day, but if there were lives to be saved, you always found Clifton at work. Matt hadn't been kidding about Clifton falling asleep on his feet. That had actually happened a few times. Clifton had been that exhausted.

Winona said, "Matt, we've got to turn Wisdom over. Could you help us?"

Wisdom was a lot heavier than he looked. Matt struggled with getting the young man turned over onto his belly.

"Thanks," Winona said.

Matt looked at Clifton. "How're you doing?"

Clifton looked incredibly old and exhausted. "I could do with another shot of whiskey. How about indulging me."

"You bet," Matt said, and he went and got him some whiskey.

The surgery went on for another hour and fifteen minutes.

She could see again.

She wasn't even sure when her sight had begun to return. All Jenna knew was that some time in the past twenty minutes or so the blackness before her eyes had gradually become gray; and the grayness became true colored vision.

Too bad there weren't many colors to see now, but tied up in the corner of a dark house on the night of a blizzard . . . well, it wasn't exactly a feast for the eyes.

Now that she no longer worried about blindness, she worried about something even simpler and more terrifying: her life.

When would Tony come up the stairs and kill her just as he'd killed Steve?

Remorse stabbed her once again. She'd been such a fool. She should never have become involved with Tony in any way.

She worked against her bonds, but they were tied very tight.

In the melodramas she was sometimes in as a young would-be actress, heroines were always escaping their fates just by wiggling their ropes back and forth until the ropes became loose.

But this wasn't a stage melodrama, and she would have no such luck.

For a long while there was only the sound of the wind in the room where Jenna was tied up.

But just then she heard somebody using the brass door knocker on the front door downstairs.

Her heart fluttered hopefully.

Had somebody come to save her at last?

She thought of Matt Ramsey, of the interest he'd seemed to take in her.

Maybe Matt was here. Maybe Matt had figured out what was going on.

Maybe Matt could figure out a way to take care of Tony and then come up here and take her ropes off.

Matt . . .

But then she heard the door slam down below and she somehow knew that it wasn't Matt at all.

• • •

"We're gonna have some fun."

"You young bastard. You remember I'm the sheriff?"

"Now how could I forget that with you wearin' a big fancy badge?"

Dowd was in the corner of the couch, glowering at Tony.

God, it was funny, seeing men who were so brave when everything was going their way and then seeing how scared they got when things went bad.

Dowd said, "You better give yourself up. While you still got a chance."

Tony laughed. "It's already too late for me."

"How's that?"

"I killed Steve and I wounded your friend Carmody."

"Carmody? The hell."

"Go take a look."

Dowd watched Tony warily, as if the outlaw might be setting a trap for the lawman.

But finally Dowd pushed himself to his feet, his fat body needing considerable effort, and then he walked out into the dining room.

In one corner he saw the stone-still body of Steve. He'd fouled himself and smelled terrible.

In the other corner he saw Carmody. Even from here he could hear the wounded man's ragged breathing. His lungs were filling up, the poor bastard, and soon enough he'd be drowning in his own fluids.

"Better get him to a doc," Dowd said.

Tony smirked. "Now don't that sound like a sensible thing to do, Dowd. I just take him over to a doc and say, yes sir, I'm the man who shot him."

"Then let me take him."

This time Tony's smirk was especially ugly. "You gave me some uncalled for shit this afternoon."

"Just doin' my duty."

"Real uncalled for shit, as a matter of fact."

"Nothin' personal in it."

Tony, who was making himself angrier as he talked, stepped up to Dowd and hit him hard in the stomach.

Dowd cried out and doubled over. He clamped his hands over his mouth.

This time Tony hit him on top of the head, driving the older man to the floor.

Tony looked at the fat slob writhing around at his feet. Tony laughed. "You better get up and get hold of yourself, Dowd. You got a long night ahead of you."

Tony paused for effect. "You and me are going to pay a visit to the bank president and then I'm going to rob the bank."

And with that, he leveled a savage kick into Dowd's back.

The man cried out again.

Bruce Laymon, the bank president, was trying to talk his wife into a little lovemaking.

By his calculation, since last January 1 they'd made love exactly seven times, and six of those times he'd had to threaten her with cutting off her allowance if she didn't perform her "wifely duty."

The fact was that Erma (Erma Mae Todd, her maiden name had been) had been raised too well by a special sect of Methodists who found sexual intercourse to be genuinely disgusting.

It was a wonder, Bruce Laymon sometimes thought, that they'd ever had the two boys. While Erma loved her children, she had not loved the moment of creating them.

So tonight the two boys were sleeping upstairs in their fine big house, while Bruce and Erma were down on the couch, cuddling under a woolen blanket and listening to the wind and snow.

"Honey?" he said.

"Huh?"

"Wouldn't it be nice?"

"Huh?"

"You know, with the wind howling and everything?"

"Oh, my Lord!"

"What?"

"I just figured out what you're talking about, Bruce."

"But snookums, it's been more than four months and—"

"Can't you hear how bad this blizzard is already?"

"Sure, but—"

"And don't you know why God sends us things like blizzards and tornadoes and—"

"Sure, but—"

"Because we're sinners and we displease him."

"I know, but—"

"So what do you want to do right in the middle of a blizzard? You want to sin even more, make Him even angrier?"

"I guess I never thought of it that way."

He'd been pressed against her, hoping his erect manliness would give her a clue or two as to what he had in mind.

But now she took his manliness and *thwacked* it with her hand, so that the pain made it go limp immediately.

"You should give him a rest," she said. "It's late and he's tired."

"Why would he be tired? He never gets any exercise."

"Let's just lie here and enjoy ourselves."

"It is a lot of fun, isn't it? Listening to a blizzard tear the town apart."

"Sarcasm is the Devil's language, and don't you forget it."

And so they sat. And listened.

He wanted to take her breasts in his hands and mouth but he knew better. He wanted to slide his leg up between her legs, but he knew better about that too.

Wind slammed against the windows. Even the roof trembled now.

He thought he would go up to sleep.

Nothing would happen now. She'd doze off.

And certainly they wouldn't have visitors.

Not this late. Not now.

Over at Carmody's, Dowd was just crawling to his feet.

"So where does the banker live?"

"He won't do it," Dowd said.

"The hell if he won't."

"Bruce Laymon's one mean sonofabitch, kid. You better know that right now."

"He won't be a mean sonofabitch when I get done with him. He'll be a dead sonofabitch, is all."

Dowd stared at the kid. No doubt about it, this one was crazier than hell, and that's just what made him so scary.

"You gonna check on Carmody?" Dowd asked.

"Nope. He's probably dead by now anyway."

"They're gonna hang you someday, kid, you wait and see."

"Well you won't be there to see it." Tony pointed his Colt right at Dowd's face. "You're gonna be a long time dead. And I'm gonna see to that personally."

And with that, he gave Dowd a shove in the direction of the front door.

Tony shrugged into his sheep-lined coat.

It was a bitch out there tonight.

CHAPTER

★13★

A few seconds after removing the third bullet from Wisdom's body, Clifton collapsed into Winona's waiting arms.

She hugged her father and held him upright so that Matt could take Clifton's arms and help him into the bedroom.

After getting him into bed and drying his sweating face and chest off with a clean towel, Winona dropped to her knees and took his hand, checking for a pulse.

Tears filling her eyes, she looked up at Matt and shook her head.

Matt clenched his jaw muscles and looked directly at his old friend's face.

It was obvious that Clifton wasn't going to be alive much longer. From the way Wisdom had been responding there at the last, it had also been obvious that Wisdom's life had been saved. His pulse was much stronger now, color was returning to his face, and when they said his name his eyelids began to flicker in recognition. He was by no means a well man yet, but he had an excellent chance of complete recovery.

Matt could only wish that Clifton had the same excellent chances.

Winona got up from her father's bedside and came over and put her face into Matt's chest.

He put his arms around her and let her cry quietly.

At one point she looked up and said, "He's not going to make it through the night, is he, Matt?"

"If anybody can, it's Clifton. Believe me."

She went back to crying.

When she was finished, she thanked Matt quietly, and together they returned to the living room, where Wisdom had been carefully covered with blankets and was now sleeping on the couch.

She checked his vital signs again. He was getting better and better.

After coming back from the kitchen with a cup of coffee, she watched curiously as Matt bundled up to go outdoors.

"You picked a strange night for an evening stroll," she said, smiling.

"I need to pay our good sheriff a visit."

"Dowd? Why?"

"Because if he didn't shoot Wisdom there, I'll bet he can tell me who did."

"Aren't you putting yourself at his mercy?"

"Not necessarily. Or at least I'm willing to take the chance."

"But he could trump up some charge and arrest you."

Matt shrugged, tugging his hat on tighter. "I'll be all right, Winona." He smiled at her. "Clifton told me that he wanted Jenna to have justice. The only man who can give her that is Dowd."

"Or Carmody."

"That's right. Or Carmody."

"Just be careful, Matt."

"Don't worry about that. I will."

And then he was out in the night.

He'd once been lost in a Montana blizzard trying to
find a valuable breeder bull that had wandered off when
the fencing had been blown down. He had that same
sense tonight. There were no streetlights, and the few
house lights that shone were faint in the blowing white
curtain that shifted constantly in front of his eyes.

He moved toward the sheriff's office. All he could
hope was that he didn't get lost.

In another part of town, Dowd was walking down the
middle of the street, slipping and sliding as he did so.
Tony kept his gun right in the lawman's back. He'd
promised to shoot Dowd if the man did anything suspicious, and both men knew that Tony would keep his
word.

Tony had no idea where they were.

Snow churned around him like a white twister. All he
could do was follow Dowd and trust that the lawman was
leading them to the banker's house.

Finally, Dowd turned around. He cupped his hands
and shouted, "It's over there."

Tony could faintly make out the outline of a two-
story Victorian home that seemed to be made out of
bricks.

"You sure that's the place?"

"I'm sure," Dowd said.

Tony motioned with his gun. "Good. Then let's get
over there."

They moved through the rustling snow, one difficult
step at a time, toward the brick home.

When they reached the small front porch, Tony saw
a kerosene lantern glow coming somewhere from the
center of the house and spilling out into the hallway.
Somebody was probably in the parlor or den.

Back at Carmody's, Tony and Dowd had rehearsed

this many times. Dowd knew just what to do.

Dowd raised a fist and knocked.

It took six knocks to bring anybody from the depths of the house.

Finally a man appeared in the door. He was dressed modestly in a robe and pajamas and carried a lantern that he held high and that cast a spooky yellow glow across his features. Behind him, Tony could see a Christmas tree, dark now but smelling sweetly. Tony had always liked Christmastime.

"Come in," Bruce Laymon said.

So Tony and Dowd stepped inside.

"Would you like to have some hot cider in the kitchen?" Laymon offered. His tone implied that he really didn't want them to but that he thought he'd ask just to be polite. Rough-hewn men like Tony and Dowd weren't exactly Bruce Laymon's social equals. At least not if you asked Bruce Laymon himself.

"Afraid we can't, Mr. Laymon," Dowd said.

Tony was amused by the servile way in which Dowd treated Laymon. It was nice to see the sheriff have to kiss a little ass.

"We came over about the bank," Dowd said.

"The bank?"

They had the man's attention immediately. He sounded as if he'd just been shot. "What about the bank?"

"Tony here found the back door open and saw two men come running out."

Laymon looked as if he were going to faint. "My God! You think it's been robbed?"

"I think that's at least a possibility. That's why I came over here. Thought you might want to go over there with us and check things out."

"Of course I do! Just give me a minute to change clothes!"

And with that he was gone, taking the lantern with him.

While they waited, Tony looked around the shadowy parlor with its fireplace and mantle and Christmas tree. This was the kind of home he'd dreamed of when he was growing up on a hard-scrabble farm in Ohio. But now the nature of his dreams had changed. He wanted a lot of good Yankee cash and he wanted the best fleshy whores that good Yankee cash could buy, and he wanted to be a big and important man. In his dreams now there was no place for a house like this and a quiet, stuffy life such as the one Bruce Laymon led.

Laymon was back in less than three minutes, huffing and puffing after moving so quickly.

He was so bundled up, with a parka and a scarf over his face, that he looked like a little kid.

Dowd led the way out.

Laymon almost got knocked over when he hit what had once been a sidewalk. He hadn't even guessed how hard the wind was coming.

They moved in single file down the street.

Tony's gun was now in his pocket but it was trained, just as before, right on the lawman's back.

And Dowd knew it, too; he knew that if he made one move that Tony didn't like the punk would kill him.

Dowd had seen many hardcases over the years, but he'd seen none who seemed as cold and determined as Tony.

They trudged on through the night on the way to the bank.

First there was pain. And then darkness. And then the sounds he made: animal sounds, the mewling sounds of a kitten who had been hurt.

Not like him to make these sounds.

Despite his cultivated manner, he was a large and durable man, a rough man really, whatever impression one might have to the contrary, and so this was unlike him.

Gunshot.

Now he remembered.

In his own home.

And the punks came in, Tony and Steve. And Jenna.

And then Tony shot him.

And then Tony shot Steve. The sonofabitch.

Carmody rolled a very small distance on his side. It hurt so tremendously. It only made the darkness all the darker, the pain.

He got one eye opened and then managed to start orienting himself.

His own home.

That's where he was.

The dining room.

Have to crawl to the kitchen. Wash up. Dress the wound. Have a shot of whiskey and . . .

He listened for Tony.

Carmody didn't want to run into that sonofabitch again unless he were armed.

He started crawling.

And crying.

The pain was that bad.

Upstairs, still working at her bonds, Jenna heard a sudden noise as somebody started moving around.

Who could it be?

Tony and Dowd had left.

And Steve was dead.

That left . . .

She'd seen Carmody shot. She had just assumed he was dead.

More noise: a chair falling over on its side.

It had to be Carmody.

Who else could it be?

By the time he'd reached the kitchen, Carmody's elbows were raw. While he'd been belly-crawling, he'd put all his weight on his elbows. Not a smart thing to do. But then he was still too dazed to be smart.

Halfway there he heard Jenna's frightened voice calling out for help. Then she stopped abruptly, apparently realizing who was down here.

There was no way that Jenna would turn to Carmody for help.

In the kitchen he managed to pull himself up to the sink.

He got hold of the pump handle and began splashing silver water into a basin.

A couple of times he thought he was going to go over backward on his feet. The wound in his side had drained him of blood and left him incredibly weak.

But now he was mad. Getting shot by some punk like Tony didn't do a lot for Carmody's self-esteem. How had a punk like Tony ever gotten into Carmody's house anyway?

And then Carmody remembered.

Jenna.

That little twist was still whining about the night he'd forced himself on her all those years ago.

And if he was really honest about it, he wasn't so sure he'd really "forced" himself anyway.

Even as a little girl, Jenna had had the look of a born whore.

So maybe Carmody had only done what somebody else would have been bound to do anyway.

Sort of break her into her natural profession.

He thought of the punk Tony again. And of how much he wanted to kill Tony. And of who was responsible for bringing him here in the first place.

And then he knew what he needed to do. Hell, *Wanted* to do.

So he started laughing.

He tore his shirt off and started cleaning the wound with soap and water. And he helped himself to a couple of staggering shots of Kentucky bourbon. And all the while he was laughing.

This time he was *really* going to give Jenna something to whine about.

He looked up and started laughing all the louder.

When they reached the bank, Tony took his gun from his pocket and put it right into Bruce Laymon's face.

"You know what this is?"

Laymon said nothing. He just glared at Dowd.

"I asked you if you knew what this was."

Above the wind, Tony could hear Laymon whisper: "Of course I do." Then: "You're the sheriff, Dowd. Are you going to let him get away with this?"

"He's got the only gun. What the hell do ya expect me to do?"

Laymon swore.

"Now, I want the three of us to go in there and I want you to go over and open the vault. And then I want the sheriff here to fill up two big mailbags with greenbacks. You understand me?"

Laymon scowled.

Tony hit him hard on the side of the jaw with the gun barrel.

Laymon reeled, almost toppling over.

"Something you should know, Mr. Laymon, and Sheriff Dowd here will tell you it's the truth: Tonight I shot two men. Killing doesn't bother me at all. Not at all. So if you try anything fancy or stupid . . ." He smiled at Laymon. "Well, I reckon you know what I'm trying to say here now, don't you?"

He pushed Laymon against the rear door of the bank.

Laymon got his key out and opened the door.

Tony stood back so Dowd and Laymon could go in first.

Once they got inside, with the door closed, the temperature went up several degrees and the keening sound of the wind died down.

It felt good to be inside.

But Tony got a little too appreciative of being indoors, because while his mind was drifting, Laymon eased himself over to a cash drawer and pulled a small handgun out of it.

But while Tony's mind was drifting elsewhere, his senses remained alert.

Just the way that Laymon started to whirl around told Tony's instincts that something was wrong here.

Tony dropped to one knee, whipped out his Colt, and fired a good clean shot into Laymon's hand.

Laymon cried out, and the gun went flying from his hand.

"You sure are one dumb sumbitch, Mr. Laymon," Tony said, grinning. "You sure are."

CHAPTER
★ 14 ★

Matt found a lone deputy at the sheriff's office. The man was hovering over a potbellied stove, drinking coffee.

"I'm looking for the sheriff."

The deputy grinned. He had dark, grimy teeth. "Ain't we all."

"You know that Deputy Wisdom's been shot?"

The deputy grinned again. "Terrible, ain't it?"

"I take it you don't care for him."

"Nobody much does around this office. He won't do what the sheriff tells him."

"You mean like break the law?"

Matt glared at the man, dropping his hand to his gun. He half wished the deputy would draw on him. Matt could get rid of a few frustrations.

From the back of the jail, he heard shouts.

The deputy laughed. "Stupid bastards."

"Who?"

The deputy shook his head. "Prisoners."

"What's wrong with them?"

"They want more blankets. The little dears is cold."

Matt believed in hanging killers and jailing criminals,

but he didn't believe in casual torture. "Maybe they are cold."

"Yeah, and I could give a shit if they are. If it's all right with you, I mean."

Matt and the deputy glared at each other.

Matt tugged his hat down low, turned his collar up again, and started out of the sheriff's office.

"You tell the sheriff I'm looking for him," Matt said.

"Yeah, and I'll bet he gets real scared."

Too bad I won't be in this town long enough to slap the shit out of this rube, Matt thought as he went back outside.

Wind and snow still lashed the streets.

He walked with his head down, pushing himself against the invisible tide that fell over him and pushed him back every few feet.

The business section of town was completely dark. Some of the buildings were buried all the way to their doorknobs.

Matt kept walking.

After a while he saw a poor dog run by, looking scared and confused and sounding miserable. Matt hoped the animal found some shelter soon. Damned soon in weather like this.

And then he saw the light on in the bank.

He walked over there, thinking maybe he'd made a mistake.

Maybe what he mistook for a light was just the way snow played off the front window.

But the closer he got, the more steadily the light glowed in the rear of the bank.

Somebody was in there.

Definitely.

And he didn't have to think long about what they'd be doing.

Actually, a blizzard would give someone all the time and protection he needed to rob a bank.

Who would be out and about to notice what a man was doing?

Matt drew his gun and walked around to the rear of the building.

She heard him coming up the steps.

He was laughing. She couldn't understand why.

She'd had no luck with the rope lashing her wrists.

If anything, the rope seemed tighter, seemed to be biting deeper and deeper into her flesh.

And then he was there.

"You little bitch," he said. "You brought those two punks here."

Jenna shrunk back against the wall.

Carmody snorted. "At least one of 'em got what he deserved."

She tried not to think of Steve. Poor, innocent, good-natured Steve.

Carmody smiled. "And now you're going to get what you deserve."

And then Jenna understood the terrible irony of all this.

She had come back to this town seeking justice for being raped when she was a little girl.

She didn't find justice. And on top of it, she was going to be raped again.

He came into the room. In the shadows she could see how messed up he looked. His entire side was bloody from where Tony had shot him.

His steps were slow, careful, as he came closer and closer to her.

"The first time you were too young to have breasts. Looks like you've got nice full ones now."

She closed her eyes and shook her head.

No. Impossible. This couldn't be happening.

Not again.

He was close enough to smell now. Sweat. Blood. And dirt from lying on the floor.

He leaned down and grabbed the top of her dress and ripped downward.

Jenna screamed.

Done with her dress, he now tore away her undergarments, so that her full breasts swung free.

"Mouthwatering," he said, and he laughed again. "Absolutely mouthwatering."

He stood up straight again, and for a silly moment she hoped that he'd decided against raping her.

Maybe, as in a melodrama she'd played in once, he'd seen his evilness and now wanted to repent.

Then she heard him fumbling with his belt.

My god.

He hadn't changed his mind at all.

"I'm gonna tell you what I told you that first time," he said, and he was quite serious about this; there was no humor in his voice now at all. "You just lie back and enjoy it. If you don't scream or kick or bite, then I won't hit you. I promise. But if you give me a hard time, you'll regret it, and I really mean that. Now, do you understand?"

She said nothing.

"I asked if you understood."

She still said nothing.

He leaned over and slapped her so hard her head slammed back against the wall.

"I don't want any trouble from you, bitch. No trouble at all."

And with that he unbuttoned his pants and let them fall to the floor.

"No trouble at all," he said as he started lowering himself to the floor.

He started talking about her mother, and she knew he was very near the end now.

Winona sat in a chair next to her father's bed. She held his hand.

"I just saw her, honey."

"Mother?"

"Yes."

"I'm happy for you, Father."

"I mean it, honey. I did. See her, I mean. She's waiting for me."

His breathing came in ragged gasps now, and when he opened his eyes she saw that their deep blue had faded. Life was leaving him.

"I want you to believe me, honey."

"I know."

"When your time comes, I want you to feel the same peace and comfort I do right now."

"I appreciate that, Father."

He looked at her, then squeezed her hand with the little remaining strength he possessed.

"I'll be there to help you over to the other side when your time comes, honey," he said.

And then he died.

It was just that sudden. And quiet. One moment he'd been alive and then . . .

She put her head to his chest and sobbed softly into the blizzard-blown night.

CHAPTER

★15★

The wind had knocked over two garbage cans behind the bank. They now scooted down the alley, banging into each other every few moments, skittering away like crazed animals.

Matt found the snowdrifts in the alley nearly impassable. He hoped he didn't have to move quickly, because that would be impossible in snow like this.

The closer he got to the back door, the more he walked in a crouched position.

There was a good chance somebody had been posted at the door and would see him coming.

He was maybe ten feet from the rear overhang when he heard the shot.

Inside the bank, Bruce Laymon grabbed his hand and cursed. Tony had expertly shot the small firearm from Laymon's hand and sent it spinning to the floor.

Laymon, watching the sullen punk move toward him, had a sudden premonition.

I will never leave this bank alive.

The thought was so overwhelming, he felt both sick to his stomach and faint.

He thought of his wife whom, despite the fact that they

rarely made love, he cared for a great deal; he thought of his two sons; and he thought of how pleasant spring would be five months hence, chestnut mares running the meadows and butterflies alighting on daisies.

He did not want to die. The thought of extinction—utter blackness for eternity—terrified him.

He felt his bowels loosen.

He would do anything the punk Tony asked.

Anything.

"I'm sorry," Laymon said.

Were those tears in his shaky voice? My god, didn't he have any dignity?

But to hell with dignity. He wanted to live. He wanted to go home and see his family.

"You try that again, Laymon, and you're dead on the spot. You understand?"

"Yes, yes, I do understand."

"Now get over to that vault and get to work."

"Please don't shoot me."

He took one step and he could feel it. He had fouled himself. My god, the warm brown stuff was running down his leg, running into the tops of his boots.

My god . . .

And then Tony started laughing.

"Hey Dowd, you know what Laymon here went and done?"

Dowd, who stood next to the vault, said, "No, and right now I don't give a damn. I just want to get this over with."

"He went and shit his pants."

"Huh?"

"Shit his pants. Just like I said."

Dowd looked at Laymon with a mixture of contempt and horror. "Don't you have no pride, man?"

Laymon was openly sobbing now. "I just want to live,

Sheriff. I don't care about anything else. I want to go home and be with my family and . . ."

Tony came up from behind Laymon and put the barrel of the gun right against the back of his skull.

"Now you go over there and get that sumbitch open, or I'm gonna kill you right on the spot. We talkin' the same language, pardner?"

"Yes, yes," Laymon said, crying. "Just please don't kill me. Please."

He eased himself over to the vault.

The way he moved, you could tell he'd shit his pants. Real careful like, trying to keep anymore of the stuff from running down his legs.

Dowd asked, "You gonna be able to open it?"

"What?"

"Lookit your hands."

And by god, old Dowd wasn't kidding.

Laymon's hands shook so badly they looked almost comic.

"Maybe you better tell me the combination and I'll do it."

"Yes. Yes, good idea," Laymon said, glancing anxiously over his shoulder to see what Tony was doing.

"We're hurrying as fast as we can," Laymon told Tony.

Tony said nothing. He just stood there with his gun pointed directly at Laymon's back.

So Laymon told Dowd the combination and Dowd went to work.

He went left the way he was supposed to, and right the way he was supposed to, and back again to the left the way he was supposed to.

And it didn't work. The goddamn safe didn't open.

"What kind've shit are you tryin' to pull here, Laymon?" Tony said.

Laymon looked as if he were literally going to fly apart. He started nervously flapping his arms and getting all big-eyed and teary-voiced again.

"That's the right combination! I swear to you, Tony! I swear to you!"

Dowd said, "Maybe I didn't hit it just right. Don't get yourself in no goddamned uproar."

"I'll get myself in an uproar if I feel like it, fatso," Tony said. "Now you git your ass back there and open that fuckin' safe."

So Dowd tried again.

And this time it worked.

Dowd picked up the kerosene lantern and walked up to the lip of the vault.

"I'll be a sumbitch," Tony said. "I done died and gone to fuckin' heaven. Yessir if I haven't."

And right then and right there he killed Laymon.

He shot the banker directly in the face, so that by the time Laymon actually hit the floor there would be this big bloody hole right where his nose and mouth had been.

This was rough even for Dowd.

"Jesus Christ," he said.

"You just get in there and start packin' that bag full of money. You understand?"

"You didn't have no cause to kill him."

"I got cause to do exactly what I feel like, old man. And you'd best remember that."

Dowd knew better than to argue.

He took the canvas bag and went in there and started loading up. It was cramped, and several times he banged his head and elbow. Tony found these moments hilarious. He had a kind of girly giggle, and it filled the entire bank.

Dowd kept working.

"How the hell you think you're gonna get out of this town?" Dowd asked him when the bag was about half filled up.

"You're gonna give me an escort."

"Huh?"

"You're gonna latch on that big-ass silver badge of yours and sit with me in a sleigh, and we're going to slide our ass right out of this burg."

"You're crazy. You know that?"

"I do seem to have heard that before. Now you git back to work."

A couple of times Dowd got some bright ideas about escaping, but each time he realized that he didn't have a chance. Not only did Tony have a gun, he also had ruthlessness on his side. He enjoyed killing people, and that was an even more formidable weapon than a gun itself.

"You about done?" Tony prodded.

"Just about."

"Then haul your ass out here, Sheriff, and bring that beautiful money with you."

Dowd still thought of Laymon. "You didn't need to kill the poor bastard. He had a family."

"You see these tears?" Tony giggled. "That's how much you're breakin' my heart."

And then the back door burst inward and there stood Matt Ramsey, his .44 pointed directly at the back of Tony's head.

"I'll kill you right on the spot if you make one move," Matt said.

And it was then that Tony spun around and opened fire on Matt.

He was lowering himself onto her.

All Jenna could do was shake her head and wonder

what dark forces in the universe would let her twice be raped by the same man.

He tore the rest of her dress and undergarments away, then paused for a look at her.

"You really are a woman now, Jenna," he said. The need was clear in his glazed eyes and in the short strokes of his breathing.

He pushed his hands between her legs and parted them.

She tried to move herself backward, get a foot up in the air and kick him. After all, only her wrists and hands were bound.

But as she twisted backward, her bottom picking up a few splinters from the floor, he grabbed her hair and slapped her across the mouth.

Once again blackness rolled before her eyes, pinpricks of light like stars in the gloom.

"Jenna," he said, "I don't want to hurt you. I really don't. I want to enjoy this. And I want you to enjoy it too. Can't you understand that? Can't you see that I'm a decent man trying to be friends with you?"

He slapped her again.

This time her head slammed against the wall behind her.

She could no longer hold her tears.

She felt as lost and abandoned as a little girl in a midnight forest.

"Now, are we going to be friends, Jenna?"

But she said nothing.

Even in her terror, she could not go along with him.

"Jenna? Did you hear me?"

Nothing.

"I want to be friends with you, Jenna."

And that was when she kicked him.

She didn't get much leverage on the kick, but she

could feel the impact when her toe reached his groin.

He sounded like a huge lumbering animal that had just been mortally shot.

He gasped and rolled over onto his side, moaning.

She scrambled to her feet.

It was not easy running with her hands bound behind her like this, but she had to get away from him.

Being raped by him a second time was something she'd never be able to endure.

She ran out of the bedroom and down the hall, looking in each room for someplace to hide.

Ah, but he'd find her easily in any of these rooms.

And she could hear him cursing her and moaning above his pain.

But soon enough he'd come lumbering out of the bedroom and start looking for her.

It was going to be even worse for her now, she knew. He was enraged now, and she didn't have to wonder who he was going to take his anger out on.

Then she saw the attic door.

She had no time to think. She had to make a quick decision.

Unable to free her hands, she backed up to the door so that she could put her hands on the doorknob and gave the knob a twist.

The door came open.

Chill attic air blasted down the stairs.

She moved quickly now, stepping inside the door, closing it gently behind her, and then quietly climbing up the stairs.

She was in darkness again. No light whatsoever.

The cold air smelled of mothballs and dust.

On one of the middle steps, she lost her balance and tripped, her forehead coming down hard against the edge of a step.

She could not allow herself the luxury of crying.

She listened to the sounds of the house below.

And then the expected noise came.

She heard him padding down the hallway below, shouting out her name amid a barrage of curses.

"You bitch! You wait till I get my hands on you!"

She heard him open doors and slam them shut. She heard furniture being slammed around. In his frenzy, he looked in places where she could not possibly be hiding: large bureau drawers and tiny closets.

Each time he failed to find her, his curses got louder and uglier.

She shuddered.

My god, if he found her this time . . .

She forced herself back to her feet and proceeded to climb the rest of the stairs.

Her head was pounding from her fall, and she could not remember ever feeling this dehydrated. She badly needed a drink of water.

But she kept climbing, climbing, until she came to the top of the stairs and stopped.

She could vaguely make out several stacks of boxes in the gloom.

They would offer her a good place to hide.

She started walking toward them, and that was when she knocked over the straight-backed chair.

Made of mahogany, the chair had blended in perfectly with the gloom. She hadn't been aware of it at all until her knee struck it.

She'd reached out for it helplessly, trying to keep it from pitching over backward, but it was too late.

The chair landed loudly against the floor.

A terrible silence ensued.

In the silence she could hear the sound echoing and echoing.

Below, his heavy footsteps stopped abruptly.

He'd heard the chair go over. No doubt about it.

Now he was trying to figure out where the sound had come from.

The silence once again.

All she could hear was the wind and the hammering of her heart.

She felt ridiculous, practically naked and with her hands bound behind her. And she felt truly helpless. She was going to be raped once more by Carmody.

She knew this with a terrible certainty.

The door at the bottom of the stairs creaked open.

He was being sly, controlling his temper.

He was not going to come rushing up here.

He was going to take his time.

She heard the door creak closed behind him. She heard his first heavy footstep on the stairway.

Oh, god.

And then she heard him laugh. Not his usual loud, almost theatrical laugh. More like a chuckle now.

"You know I'm here, don't you, bitch?" he said. "You know I'm coming up the stairs, don't you?"

Oh, god.

All she could do was crouch behind the stack of boxes and close her eyes and hurl desperate prayers into the dark, indifferent universe.

CHAPTER

★ 16 ★

Matt shot Tony twice in the face and once in the chest. The gunman spun around completely, then fell facefirst to the floor. Matt could hear his nose snapping when it hit the linoleum-covered boards.

Dowd said, "I'll be goddamned, Ramsey. You're one hell of a shot."

Dowd was behind Matt now.

When he stepped forward from the shadows, he put a gun directly against the back of Matt's skull.

"Drop your gun, Reb, elsewise I'm gonna put a big hole in your head."

"You're done in this town, Dowd, and you know it. Killing me won't buy you anything."

"Maybe it'll buy me some satisfaction, Reb. If you hadn't come to town none of this would have happened."

"That's where you're wrong. If it hadn't been me, it would have been somebody else. You can't run a show like this all your life."

"I told you to throw your gun down, Reb."

The lawman eased back on the hammer.

The sound was loud in the bank.

"You hear me, you Reb sonofabitch?"

So Matt threw his gun down.

The two corpses had begun to smell.

The wind was still threatening to tear the roof off.

Matt wondered how long he had before the pudgy sheriff eased his finger back on the trigger and dispatched Matt to the great and abiding darkness that scared the hell out of most human beings.

Matt thought of his brother Amos and his bride Rose Margaret, who still lived in Fannin County, along with their four kids; of Luke, the second youngest, who'd just wed a Jack County girl; of Kyle off in Colorado, hoping to strike it rich; and of the mother and father and teenage sister Matt had to bury just after the war, thanks to the killing skills of Kiowa raiders battling cattle rustlers.

Life held so many disappointments a man sometimes wondered if he could hold up against them.

For instance, now.

There was a very good chance this old lard ass was going to actually shoot Matt down in cold blood. Dowd would come up with some story that justified the killing.

So Matt starting thinking: What the hell. I may as well go out in glory.

Dowd pulled the hammer even farther back.

"This is gonna hurt like a sonofabitch," the lawman said. "My oh my."

"Just get it over with."

"You makin' like you ain't scared?"

"I'm not makin' like anything. I just want you to get it over with."

"You're just like Laymon. Any second now you're gonna start shittin' your pants."

Dowd pulled the hammer back even more.

"Part of your head's gonna be slidin' down that wall over there," Dowd said. "Messy goddamn way to kill a guy, I have to confess."

"Just pull it," Matt said.

And then he dove in a arc for the large desk to the right of the safe.

Dowd squeezed off a couple of shots, but Matt was able to elude them by rolling away.

"You sonofabitch," Dowd said, sounding like a kid whose fun had been spoiled by a playmate.

Matt snatched a book off the corner of the desk and pitched it at the kerosene lamp that sat glowing atop a desk closer to the vault.

Dowd snapped off two more shots in the sudden darkness. The flames from his gun were orange-red in the gloom, and they smelled of heavy gunpowder.

"You still ain't gettin' out of here, Reb."

Matt said nothing.

He started crawling from around the desk.

He accidentally nudged a wastepaper basket. He swore silently at his own clumsiness.

Dowd fired two loud shots at the basket.

In the darkness, Matt stopped. He had to be careful. Bad a shot as Dowd was, he could still get lucky.

Matt started crawling again.

Dowd said, "Be easier if you just gave yourself up. Maybe we can make some kind of deal, Reb. Maybe I won't have to kill you after all."

Matt smiled to himself. The old bastard was getting scared. The whining wind and the darkness in the bank were kind of scary, and Dowd was getting spooked.

For no apparent reason at all, the lawman let loose with another couple of volleys.

The bank interior resonated with the defeaning noise.

Because of the shots, Matt now knew where Dowd was standing.

He knew now that he'd get his chance at the old man after all.

Still crawling, Matt swung wide behind the desk nearest the vault.

Dowd stood on the other side of the same desk.

If Matt could just ease himself up and . . .

"That was a serious offer, Reb, about you surrenderin' and everything, I mean."

The old bastard's voice was trembling.

There was no better time to move than now.

And so Matt leapt over the desk, grabbing the lawman around the neck so hard he thought he might have snapped it.

The lawman shouted for help and then proceeded to put up an impressive struggle.

Matt got hold of Dowd's gun hand and slapped the gun away. He then drove a right cross into the man's chest and a hard left into the man's heart.

Dowd started to sink to the floor, but not before Matt had caught him with a right cross.

Dowd went over backward, a chair collapsing beneath him on his way down.

Matt scrambled in the darkness to find his gun. When he had it, he went over to the lawman and said, "You think Carmody's still at his place?"

"You gonna shoot me, Reb?"

"You didn't answer my question."

"Yeah. He's there, I'm sure."

"Get up."

"Huh?"

"You heard me."

"What for?"

"Just do what I say."

The lawman stood up. Matt slapped him viciously across the mouth.

He reached over to the lawman's belt and snapped the handcuffs free.

He reached up and got Dowd by the collar, then hauled him over to a support post that ran floor to ceiling in the rear of the bank.

He had to work in darkness, but he didn't want to take time to light the lamp again.

He took Dowd's arms and wrapped them around the post.

"The key?"

"Huh?"

"For the handcuffs."

"Oh."

"Where is it?"

"In my left coat pocket."

Matt dug in and got it.

He handcuffed the lawman to the post.

"I'll freeze my ass off in here tonight."

"That's a pretty sad story, you crooked old bastard," Matt said.

"You really gonna leave me here?"

Matt laughed. "Hell yes, I am."

"You sonofabitch," Dowd said.

By now Matt was used to people in this town calling him names.

He ran out the door, headed for Carmody's.

CHAPTER
17

Jenna could see him at the top of the stairs. Carmody. Like some huge, blind monster, feeling its way through the gloom.

It would only be a matter of minutes before he found her hiding behind the boxes, and for the second time in her life, he would . . .

"I'm only going to be madder if I have to keep looking for you, Jenna."

She crouched even lower behind the boxes. Her nose had started to itch. The dust was very bad for her sinuses.

"I won't hurt you. All I want is your body for a few minutes, Jenna. I didn't hurt you the last time, did I, Jenna?"

He tried to sound reasonable and patient. This only made him sound all the more sinister.

"Come on now, Jenna. Just tell me where you are."

He started walking.

He started way over on the westward side, the farthest point from Jenna.

He bumped into things. Instead of cursing, however, he laughed.

"This is like hide-and-go-seek," he said. "It's like

we're kids again, Jenna, playing a nice little game."

She wanted to start sobbing. She wasn't even sure why.

"Jenna, Jenna, where are you?"

He slammed into something else.

This time he made a sound of pain. And this time he did curse.

She wished she had clothes on. Maybe then she wouldn't feel so vulnerable.

And then she sneezed.

She couldn't believe it.

No warning whatsoever; she just suddenly sneezed.

Carmody laughed. "Oh, Jenna, I don't have to tell you what kind of trouble you're in now, do I?"

She wanted to slap herself for helping him find her.

"Jenna."

She hunched even farther over. Her heart beat so loudly in her ears she imagined he could hear it too.

"Jenna."

And then he was there, over her, hurling boxes out of his way with great and thunderous strength, staring down hungrily at her half-naked body.

"Hello, Jenna. Ready for a little fun?"

She screamed and tried to run. But he was very fast, Carmody was, and in half a moment he had hold of her by her hair.

"I'm sure ready for some fun, Jenna," he said, pulling her up to him. "And I sure hope you are too."

Matt slipped three times on his way to Carmody's house.

A coating of ice had glazed the snow, making walking even more treacherous.

He knew Jenna was in trouble.

So he hurried. And slipped.

By the time he reached the large estate, he was angry enough to just assault the door.

To his surprise, the house was unlocked.

He went inside, his .44 leading the way.

The interior smelled of carnage. He thought of a hog kill on a hot windless day. This was even worse than that.

He found Steve dead, and in the dining room he saw where another body had lain, its outline drawn in its own blood.

Carmody.

And then he heard the screaming.

He didn't have to wonder who it was. Or what was happening to her.

For the second time in her life, Jenna was about to be raped by Carmody.

Matt went up the stairs two at a time. He stood on the second-floor landing, gaping around, listening.

He ran down the hallway, searching rooms but turning up nothing.

Where had the scream come from?

And then she cried out again.

Matt ran back to the hallway. The way the wind had swallowed up the scream, he still couldn't be exactly certain where she was.

And then he saw the door that was opened only a tiny crack.

He ran to it, threw it back, and looked up the attic stairs.

Of course. That's where she was.

He took these stairs two at a time as well.

Just when he reached the top, however, he heard Jenna shout, "He's got a gun, Matt."

And just as he tried to find some kind of protection in the inky blackness, a gun roared through the shadows,

and tracers of yellow flame went right past his head and
dug into the wall behind him.

"You come any closer, Ramsey," Carmody said, "and
I'll kill her."

Matt listened as Carmody swept Jenna up and clutched
her to him as a shield.

Carmody knocked over boxes as he dragged Jenna,
kicking and cursing him, toward the stairs.

Matt was almost shocked to see that Jenna was nearly
naked. Large bruises showed themselves over most of
her body. He had to wonder if Carmody had already
succeeded.

Carmody got them to the top of the stairs. Matt stood
only a few feet away.

All three of them were panting, and their breathing
was loud and ragged in the stillness.

"I'm going to take her downstairs with me," Carmody
said, "and if you try one thing, Ramsey, I'm going to put
a fucking hole in her. You understand?"

Matt nodded.

"Now come on, bitch, let's get rolling."

Carmody yanked Jenna around so that she was behind
him. If Matt was tempted to shoot, he'd only end up
killing Jenna.

Carmody started down the stairs, dragging her.

Jenna whimpered and moaned.

"Shut up, bitch," Carmody said.

And then Jenna screamed, "Now, Matt!"

At first, given the deep shadows, it wasn't easy to
see what Jenna had done, but after a few moments he
saw that she'd hurled herself down the steps so that she
would knock Carmody off his feet.

Carmody's gun misfired. In the small stairway, the
roar was ear-shattering.

He tried to scramble to his feet, but Matt was already

there, leaping over Jenna and pushing his gun right into Carmody's face.

And somewhere behind him, he heard Jenna start to cry, and he heard in her tears how the rape at nine years old had destroyed her life.

She would never quite be a whole person, even if Matt took the trouble to pistol-whip Carmody right here and now.

Matt did give in to one temptation.

Carmody was stuck about halfway down the stairs.

Matt gave him a shove.

The big man tumbled over and over himself all the way down to the second-floor landing.

Matt went over and took off his warm coat and gave it to Jenna.

He went over and cocked the steel-tipped toe of his boot and kicked Carmody right in the stomach.

Carmody cried out.

"That's gonna feel real good, compared to the way that rope's going to feel around your neck," Matt said.

CHAPTER
★18★

Two days later, Matt stood in the living room of Clifton Ruark's house

Wisdom, all bandaged up, freshly shaven and wearing a new western-style shirt with nice imitation pearl buttons, said, "I owe you a big favor, Matt."

"You owe nothing, except being the best sheriff you know how to be."

Winona smiled. You could tell that her father's death was still her main preoccupation, but every few minutes she'd force herself back to the present. "He's going to make a fine sheriff, Matt. Don't let him kid you."

And then they all turned to look at Jenna.

Matt said, "How about you, Jenna? Have you decided what you're doing next?"

The young woman still bore a black eye from Carmody's fist. "Probably go east somewhere and set up an acting school."

"Oh really?" Winona said, sounding genuinely interested.

Jenna shrugged. "I think my traveling days are over. I'm looking forward now to settling down."

Wisdom grinned. "How about you, Matt? Does settling down sound good to you yet?"

Matt laughed. "Not quite yet. But pretty soon I imagine I'll get tired of bedrolls and campfires and want to settle in."

Wisdom winked. "Bedrolls and campfires sound pretty good to me. Course, that may be because I'm about to get married." And then he looked at Winona. "Right?"

"Absolutely right, Sheriff Wisdom," Winona said.

"Well," Matt said, putting on his hat, "the stage is leaving and I reckon it's time that Jenna and I get down to it."

Warm sunlight had begun to melt the snow. Word was that travel over the roads and through the passes was possible again.

"Wish you could stay for supper," Winona said.

Jenna and Winona embraced. "Wish I could too," Jenna said.

And then they were out the door, in the snappy but not chill weather, walking toward the business district and the stage depot.

After they'd gone a few feet, she said, "It's over."

"Pardon me?"

"I came back here to settle something in my past. And you know what?"

"What?"

She looked at him and smiled. "I settled it. And now it's over. And now I want to go on with my life."

Matt had never seen Jenna happy before. It was a right nice experience.

A special offer for people who enjoy reading the best Westerns published today. If you enjoyed this book, subscribe now and get ...

TWO FREE

A $5.90 VALUE—NO OBLIGATION

If you enjoyed this book and would like to read more of the very best Westerns being published today, you'll want to subscribe to True Value's Western Home Subscription Service. If you enjoyed the book you just read and want more of the most exciting, adventurous, action packed Westerns, subscribe now.

Each month the editors of True Value will select the 6 very best Westerns from America's leading publishers for special readers like you. You'll be able to preview these new titles as soon as they are published, FREE for ten days with no obligation.

TWO FREE BOOKS

When you subscribe, we'll send you your first month's shipment of the newest and best 6 Westerns for you to preview. With your first shipment, two of these books will be yours as our introductory gift to you absolutely FREE, regardless of what you decide to do. If you like them, as much as we think you will, keep all six books but pay for just 4 at the low subscriber rate of just $2.45 each. If you decide to return them, keep 2 of the titles as our gift. No obligation.

Special Subscriber Savings

When you become a True Value subscriber you'll save money several ways. First, all regular monthly selections will be billed at the low subscriber price of just $2.45 each. That's

WESTERNS!

at least a savings of $3.00 each month below the publishers price. Second, there is never any shipping, handling or other hidden charges—Free home delivery. What's more there is no minimum number of books you must buy, you may return any selection for full credit and you can cancel your subscription at any time. A TRUE VALUE!

Mail the coupon below

To start your subscription and receive 2 FREE WESTERNS, fill out the coupon below and mail it today. We'll send your first shipment which includes 2 FREE BOOKS as soon as we receive it.

Mail To:
True Value Home Subscription Services, Inc.   10668
P.O. Box 5235
120 Brighton Road
Clifton, New Jersey 07015-5235

YES! I want to start receiving the very best Westerns being published today. Send me my first shipment of 6 Westerns for me to preview FREE for 10 days. If I decide to keep them, I'll pay for just 4 of the books at the low subscriber price of $2.45 each; a total of $9.80 (a $17.70 value). Then each month I'll receive the 6 newest and best Westerns to preview Free for 10 days. If I'm not satisfied I may return them within 10 days and owe nothing. Otherwise I'll be billed at the special low subscriber rate of $2.45 each; a total of $14.70 (at least a $17.70 value) and save $3.00 off the publishers price. There are never any shipping, handling or other hidden charges. I understand I am under no obligation to purchase any number of books and I can cancel my subscription at any time, no questions asked. In any case the 2 FREE books are mine to keep.

Name _____

Address _____ Apt. # _____

City _____ State _____ Zip _____

Telephone # _____

Signature _____
(if under 18 parent or guardian must sign)
Terms and prices subject to change.
Orders subject to acceptance by True Value Home Subscription Services, Inc.